Someone was following them.

Dunne pulled the gun out of his pack. When he turned, he was momentarily surprised to find Quinn holding a gun of her own.

"Where'd you get that?"

She actually laughed at him. "Do I strike you as the kind of woman who goes unarmed into anything? And before you ask, I'm an excellent shot."

He hoped she was right and not overly confident. "Keep close. You walk forward, I'll be at your six. We'll stay on our path."

She nodded and moved in front of him. He followed, his back facing hers so they weren't ambushed. Eventually they made it to the clearing where the murder happened.

"Dunne."

He turned. She was pointing at something.

There was an arrow stuck in a tree a few yards away. Something was stuck to the tree with the arrow.

It was an envelope. With his name on it.

He tore open the envelope. Inside was a small sheet of paper with a few simple words typed in a haunted-house-type font.

WELCOME. LET THE GAMES BEGIN.

CASING THE COPYCAT

—

Nicole Helm

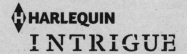

To my grandpa Bob, whose unexplained creepy newspaper
clipping binder inspired the Eye Socket Killer.

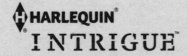

HARLEQUIN®
INTRIGUE™

Recycling programs
for this product may
not exist in your area.

ISBN-13: 978-1-335-58259-1

Casing the Copycat

Copyright © 2023 by Nicole Helm

For questions and comments about the quality of this book,
please contact us at CustomerService@Harlequin.com.

Harlequin Enterprises ULC
22 Adelaide St. West, 41st Floor
Toronto, Ontario M5H 4E3, Canada
www.Harlequin.com

Printed in U.S.A.

Nicole Helm grew up with her nose in a book and the dream of one day becoming a writer. Luckily, after a few failed career choices, she gets to follow that dream—writing down-to-earth contemporary romance and romantic suspense. From farmers to cowboys, Midwest to *the* West, Nicole writes stories about people finding themselves and finding love in the process. She lives in Missouri with her husband and two sons, and dreams of someday owning a barn.

Books by Nicole Helm

Harlequin Intrigue

Covert Cowboy Soldiers

The Lost Hart Triplet
Small Town Vanishing
One Night Standoff
Shot in the Dark
Casing the Copycat

A North Star Novel Series

Summer Stalker
Shot Through the Heart
Mountainside Murder
Cowboy in the Crosshairs
Dodging Bullets in Blue Valley
Undercover Rescue

A Badlands Cops Novel

South Dakota Showdown
Covert Complication
Backcountry Escape
Isolated Threat
Badlands Beware
Close Range Christmas

Visit the Author Profile page at Harlequin.com.

CAST OF CHARACTERS

Dunne (Wilks) Thompson—Trained army medic, now ranching in Wilde, Wyoming. Walks with a limp due to an injury during his final mission. His grandfather was a known serial killer, and Dunne is determined to find the man who's currently acting as a copycat killer.

Quinn Peterson—Grew up in an off-the-grid cult. Was saved from said cult by her identical twin and the Thompson brothers. Injured from saving her identical twin from a gunshot. Bored due to her injury, so she wants to help Dunne solve his mystery.

Jessie Peterson—Quinn's identical twin, who did not know Quinn existed until they came into contact a few months ago. Living at the ranch with Henry Thompson.

Sarabeth Peterson—Jessie's eleven-year-old daughter.

Henry Thompson—Dunne's former military brother, currently ranching with the other Thompson brothers. In a relationship with Jessie.

Zara and Hazeleigh Hart—Sisters. Thompson Ranch was originally their family's property. Zara is engaged to Jake Thompson. Hazeleigh is dating Landon Thompson.

Jake, Landon and Cal Thompson—The remaining Thompson brothers who all ranch together after they had to take on new lives after a terrorist group unearthed their real identities back when they were in the military.

Chapter One

Quinn Peterson was no stranger to injury. Growing up the way she had—raised in off-the-grid compounds run by what could only be termed "sociopathic, murderous psychopaths"—she'd been beaten, bruised, stabbed, twice, and shot, once, though just a flesh wound in the arm.

Her *current* gunshot wound had been in the upper thigh, and though a few weeks had passed since the night she'd stepped in front of a gunman to save her sister's life, it still hurt like hell.

She hated it.

Everyone kept telling her she was *lucky*. The bullet had missed her femur and wasn't that a miracle?

It hadn't felt like one—then or now.

She hated physical therapy almost as much as she hated an eleven-year-old teaching her how to read—because she was almost thirty years old and she'd never had an opportunity to learn.

Somehow, Sarabeth—her wily little niece—had figured out Quinn's embarrassing secret, and instead of blabbing to everyone, she'd set out to teach Quinn on the down low.

God, Quinn loved that little girl. She even loved her sister, who she'd only just really gotten to know these past few weeks. She'd never admit it, but this was the family she'd been searching for her entire life.

She didn't *belong* in it of course. Not really. She should be dead or in jail like all the men who'd "raised" her, but she'd taken a bullet for Jessie. Based on how everyone around the ranch acted, that meant she'd earned a get-into-the-family-free card.

Quinn Peterson had never been stupid enough to look a gift horse in the mouth.

Except maybe the one standing before her in the shape of a tall, built ex-soldier who had a blank expression on his objectively beautiful face.

Dunne Thompson *always* had a blank expression.

The problem with Dunne, former combat medic and current rancher, was that nothing riled him. Literally nothing. When she'd spent a lifetime learning how to rile everyone around her so they didn't get too close.

Dunne never reacted—not to her jokes, her barbs, her insults, her outrageous innuendo. He kept that blank-faced calm in every situation.

It made her bound and determined to find a crack in that very impressive, and handsome, armor.

"Am I going to have a limp forever, like you?" she asked, resolutely not doing the exercise he'd just instructed her to do in his little torture chamber of a room. The room in the back of the Thompson ranch house was big and had likely once acted as some kind of parlor, but had recently been adapted into Dunne's bedroom.

Which also served as his medical facility. She supposed you could take the combat medic out of combat, but the medic part of him still survived.

"If you don't do your physical therapy," Dunne said, not at all affected by her quip about his limp.

One of these days… *One* of these days, she was going to find that Achilles' heel. But for right now, she had to find a way out of the exercise, which hurt and made her feel weak and stupid.

She hated looking weak in front of anyone, but Dunne always somehow made it into a kind of contest. He, *of course*, had suffered a femur break, so he didn't appreciate her whining. *He'd* had to be airlifted out of a war zone. *She'd* only ridden in an ambulance to a nice hospital.

"Lift your leg, Quinn."

"I don't get it. I'm shot. I should be *resting*. Healing. Doesn't everyone say rest is part of healing?"

"Only people who don't know what they're talking about. I was running a mile this long after my injury, and mine was far worse."

"You know, I find this whole manly pissing match over the size of our war wounds fun and all, but you always win."

"That I do. Lift your leg."

She groaned, poked at him a few times, but eventually lifted her damn leg. She'd never met a thicker, harder-headed brick wall than Dunne.

It was *infuriating*.

When they were done, he didn't give her a "good

job." Didn't say much of anything except that he expected her back for their evening session after dinner.

She had a million obnoxious retorts to that, but the less he reacted, the less she used them.

When she figured out how to get past his icy veneer, it was going to be *good*.

So she left him in his stupid little room and tried to think of ways to really get under his skin while she hunted Sarabeth down for their next reading lesson.

She needed to find something out about him. Something personal. Something he wouldn't expect her to know.

Usually Sarabeth was back from the stables by now, but the girl did love those animals, so Quinn decided to go sit on the side porch off the kitchen and wait for Sarabeth to appear.

Wyoming was starting to ease its way into summer, and this little corner of it—the Thompson Ranch—was pretty as a picture, with the small cabin across the yard and the mountains in the distance, beyond all the pasture dotted with cows. The only thing that marred the visual was the stables, which were being rebuilt after suffering severe fire damage a few weeks back.

Quinn rubbed at her leg where the bullet had gone. She considered it something like a penance. She'd done plenty of bad in her life. But she'd saved Jessie's life, and for that, she could be proud.

She blew out a breath. *Proud.* A bit of a stretch.

Bitterness wanted to spread, but she refused to let it. She turned to head back inside. She'd let Sarabeth find her. She'd go do something productive. Something…

Quinn stopped at the screen door. She heard lowered voices and it was something like a habit to eavesdrop. Men huddling together whispering? A smart woman stopped, hid and listened so she didn't end up dead in a ditch somewhere.

Quinn stood where she was hidden enough by the screen door so they wouldn't see her, but she could hear everything.

Henry moved into her sight line first, opening the door down to the basement. As far as Quinn knew, there wasn't much down there. It wasn't finished. It was just storage.

But Dunne came into view, his normal stoic expression just a little…different. Tighter, somehow. She watched him with great interest as he nodded at Henry and then took the first, careful step down the stairs.

Dunne tended to avoid stairs if he could. They were hard on his leg. So what were the Thompson brothers doing sneaking around somewhere one of them didn't like to go?

Quinn stayed where she was, still hidden, watching the now closed basement door. Maybe when they came back up—

"Oh, there you are."

Quinn nearly jumped a foot, which caused a searing pain to shoot through her leg. She looked over her shoulder at Sarabeth, who was cradling a little black kitten at the bottom of the side porch stairs.

"My chores are done. Want to do your next lesson?" Sarabeth asked, clearly unaware she'd startled Quinn.

"Shh. It's supposed to be a secret, remember?"

Sarabeth bit her lip and wrinkled her nose. "About that…"

Jessie swept into the kitchen from the living room, a stack of books in her arms. "Come and sit at the table," she instructed, waving Quinn and Sarabeth inside as she put the books down. "I didn't keep a lot of Sarabeth's old books since we moved around a bunch, but Hazeleigh said there were some things in the attic. These should work."

Quinn glared at Sarabeth even as she held the door open for her. "You *told*?"

"I didn't *mean* to." Sarabeth slipped past her and into the kitchen.

"Uh-uh," Jessie said, waving her finger at Sarabeth and the cat. "Henrietta is *not* allowed in the kitchen, and you know that, young lady."

Sarabeth pouted, but she walked through the kitchen, speaking in low tones to the cat as she likely went to secret the cat away in her room.

Quinn stayed where she was on the porch, though she still held the door open. Too many complex emotions were worming around in her stomach. She hated that Jessie knew she couldn't read.

Jessie'd had it rough too, but she'd had a somewhat normal childhood for a little bit, living with their grandmother rather than at their father's compound. At least until she'd been a teenager.

Jessie smiled at her through the screen. "She tried to lie. Really, she did."

Quinn grunted and stepped inside. The more she acted like it was a big deal, the more Jessie would make her feel like an embarrassed idiot. Better to pretend it didn't matter.

She flopped into the chair but then looked around the kitchen, which was so often the center for everything. A million people coming and going because the Thompsons had a little compound of their own among the six of them plus four of those six shacking up with someone. One of those someones coming with an eleven-year-old daughter.

No one seemed to mind the tight quarters. Everyone seemed to *enjoy* it.

And likely, someone would come waltzing in and wonder why the hell she was looking at kids' books.

"I don't want anyone knowing about this," she muttered, slumping in her chair.

"No one would—" Quinn made a move to get up because she didn't want placating baloney, but Jessie grabbed her hand. "Okay, no one else will know. I promise. I'll go put the books away and we'll work on it after dinner. In your room."

"You're going to tell Henry." Because Quinn might not know how love worked, but she knew Jessie wasn't going to lie to the man she loved.

"I'll be vague." She smiled reassuringly. "I'll just say I'm helping you with catching up on some things."

Quinn knew it was only because she'd taken the bullet meant for Jessie that Jessie was so nice to her. It was the only reason *anyone* was nice to her. But Jessie sometimes made her wish that it could be…more. Like a real sister thing instead of just guilt or gratitude.

Sarabeth clamored back into the kitchen. She frowned at Jessie and Quinn's clasped hands.

"When can *I* get a sister?" Sarabeth asked gustily.

Jessie nearly choked.

Quinn grinned, glad to have the attention off herself. She looked at Jessie. "Yeah, all this shacking up together. Shouldn't there be a ring and a baby on the way?"

"Thanks a lot," Jessie muttered under her breath.

Quinn chuckled, but since Jessie was being nice, Quinn figured she could be too. She changed the subject from sisters and rings before Sarabeth grabbed on to the topic too tightly "What do the guys do downstairs?"

"Downstairs?" Jessie returned. She seemed surprised, but if Quinn had to guess, it wasn't about them *being* downstairs, but about Quinn *knowing* they were downstairs.

"Yeah, in that creepy old basement. They're down there right now."

"Who is?"

"Dunne and Henry."

"Hmm. Well." Jessie glanced up as the screen door screeched open. "Oh no, Zara. What happened?"

Zara Hart—ranch hand to the Thompson brothers and engaged to one of them—came in, holding a dirty rag to her arm. The rag was covered in dirt, grease and blood. "A fight with barbed wire. The barbed wire won."

Jessie moved to help clean Zara up and Quinn had

no doubt the conversation about the basement was deemed over.

But that only made Quinn determined to get to the bottom of it.

DUNNE THOMPSON LOOKED at the makeshift mission board he'd put together with facts and information he'd been gathering for years. He'd meant to always keep it to himself. A morbid kind of fascination in what he'd come from.

But the past few months, things had changed, because while his grandfather was dead, someone out there was killing people just like his grandfather had done back in the 1950s and '60s.

It didn't have anything to do with Dunne. So his grandfather had been a serial killer? Shit happened. But somehow this copycat killer...got under his skin. Made him feel like he had to do something to stop it.

So, he'd brought in Cal. Then Henry. And now all five of his military brothers knew about the copycat Eye Socket Killer—known for taking the eyeballs of his victims.

Dunne knew it wasn't his responsibility per se, but it haunted him. He wanted to find a way to put an end to it. Whether it was finding something he could send off to the police investigating or whether it was handling it himself.

"The case is getting more high-profile now," Henry said, sounding grim. "News outlets are starting to surmise he's out to kill someone in every state."

"There's only been seven," Jake pointed out, frowning at one of Dunne's many binders of news coverage over the first wave of Eye Socket murders. "They really think there's forty-plus more to go?"

"Or there's a handful they haven't found yet," Dunne said flatly.

"I know we've said it before, but it bears repeating. This isn't your responsibility, Dunne."

Dunne didn't look at Cal. They had all said it to him at one point or another, and Dunne knew they were right. But knowing and feelings were two very different things. "It's not a responsibility. It's more…" An ingrained *need*. "It's something to do, anyway."

"Not exactly the lying low we're supposed to be doing," Cal continued, but it wasn't with the same irritable disgust he'd had in their first few months here.

Dunne had never pictured himself as a rancher in the middle of nowhere, Wyoming. A military brat didn't know what to do with a town with roots so tangled and deep you couldn't walk down the street without tripping over them.

Of course, he'd never pictured himself fighting terrorists and taking down entire organizations, or having to die—on paper—and become someone else.

Well, truth be told, ever since he'd found out about his grandfather in the ninth grade, he'd definitely dreamed about being someone else.

Now he got to be, so why was he obsessing over this? Like Cal said, it wasn't his responsibility.

"I'll look into what the police have and the media don't on this new one," Landon offered since he was an expert with computers and hacking into systems without being traced.

"Thanks."

They went over the new details and added them to the board, then his brothers started making their excuses. Henry had promised to take Sarabeth on a ride. Jake had promised to go check the north fences with Zara. Hazeleigh was making Landon lunch, and Brody made some lame excuse about barn chores, which sounded to Dunne a lot like a reason to sneak off to spend time with Kate—though they shared a room and a life so Dunne didn't see why he'd need to.

Cal was the only one who stayed down with him, because Cal was the only one who didn't have anything pressing to do that involved other people.

"Think we're going to hold out?" Dunne asked, desperate to think about anything unrelated to murder.

"Hold out what?"

"The whole love bug. I wasn't worried until Henry fell. Next thing you know, you'll have a wife, two kids and a dog."

Cal didn't snort derisively like Dunne had expected him to, but he did scowl. "We'll hold out just fine." He slid Dunne a look. "And maybe even stop a serial killer while we do."

Dunne managed a smile.

What else was there to do?

Chapter Two

Quinn didn't stop mulling over the mysterious basement meeting. They'd all been down there, coming up at different times, acting like it was some grave secret why they'd be downstairs.

Clearly the women in the house who lived with them knew what was going on. Zara didn't seem like the type to let her fiancé wander about without knowing exactly what he was doing.

Quinn enjoyed watching the couples, the brothers, the way all the different people dealt with each other. She'd always been good at figuring folks out. She had most of them down to a T.

Except the man currently walking her through her physical therapy exercises.

And since she didn't understand him and didn't care about tiptoeing around people's secrets, she went ahead and just asked. "What do you guys do in the basement?"

He didn't respond in any way. Not a flinch, not a blink of surprise. He stood there as stoic as ever.

It made her want to punch him. Or wish she could go back in time and shoot him when she'd had the chance.

"Basement is just storage," he said evenly.

But he made her so crazy she was overanalyzing the pause between her voicing the question and him answering. Did it mean something? When she knew he *always* took his time to answer questions?

She should have known better to ask then, because *of course* he wasn't going to tell her. It was some kind of big secret, and she didn't really belong here or deserve anyone trusting her with secrets.

Didn't mean she was satisfied with being all but lied to. Still, she didn't ask him any more questions while he talked her through her physical therapy exercises. Once he was satisfied, he dismissed her.

Like she was some subordinate soldier and he was master supreme general of the whole world.

She bit back her nasty retort though. She stepped out of his room without saying a thing.

Her leg ached, and she was a little sweaty from all the exercises she'd had to do, but that wasn't going to stop her.

No one was in the kitchen. Dunne had closed his door behind her. There was only her.

And the door to the basement.

If he didn't tell her, why couldn't she go find out for herself? Besides, they'd *insisted* she'd live here. Well, Jessie had and then Henry had and then his brothers had, but still...

Didn't she deserve to know what was going on in the house she was living in? She'd spent her entire life in compounds of men and secrets and violence.

She damn well deserved to know if she was surrounded by something shady.

She was done with shady. She might not be the best, nicest person in the world, but she was done with bad and evil and...violent. She wanted a normal, safe life.

Okay, maybe not *normal*. That sounded boring. But safe sounded good. Important.

She marched to the door and carefully pulled it open so it didn't squeak too loud. She stepped into the dark, and pulled the door shut behind her before she flipped on the light.

She took the first step down, trying not to wince at the pain in her leg or the creaking noise the board made under her feet.

Well, if someone asked her why she was down here, she's just claim physical therapy. Steps were basically exercising her leg, right?

She made it to the bottom of the stairs and frowned. The lone light bulb flickered, casting everything in an eerie glow, but it was just...storage. Boxes. Cartons of ranch equipment. Tools. She moved through the rows of neatly organized ranch excess, eyebrows drawn together.

What the hell did they come down here for then?

She was about to head back upstairs when something odd caught the corner of her eye. A big...thing. A flat thing on wheels. She didn't have the slightest clue what something like that would be used for, so she went over to inspect it.

When she pulled it, it rolled easily and on the other side was a bulletin board. Huge. And there were all sorts of news articles, timelines, maps and pictures pinned to it. Pictures of dead bodies with their eyeballs removed.

"A hell of a time to not be able to read," she muttered. Because *yikes.* Still, she'd seen dead bodies in real life. A few pictures didn't affect her too much.

She picked one article and tried to sound out the headline. It took a while, but she finally thought she got it.

"Eye Socket Killer Strikes Again."

Well, that explained the pictures, she supposed.

Even though she'd dealt with plenty of bad men and murderers, something about that awful name matched with the pictures sent a shudder through her. She struggled through reading the first sentence and only got the basic gist that a body had been found with its eyes removed.

Apparently it wasn't the first one.

What was this? Were the Thompson brothers some sort of pack of serial killers? This was their hideout and planning station? They were six psychotic murderers. Were there jars of eyeballs hidden around the basement?

She laughed. Couldn't help it. No, of course not. She rarely believed the best of people, but she also knew what the Thompson brothers had done to protect Jessie and Sarabeth and even her. They weren't murderers, or at least, not the creepy, planned, serial killer kind.

So, what was all this? It was like one of those detective shows, she supposed. Which meant they were probably *tracking* a serial killer.

Probably trying to stop one, knowing this six.

There was just *so* much information. The board. A pile of binders hidden behind it. Years of work or research or something.

It wasn't all that different from her father and uncle obsessed with finding some old treasure. It was fixation. It was compulsion.

Maybe this was for a good cause, but it still wasn't normal, healthy behavior to have all this information about a serial killer.

She moved on to another article. She ran her finger over the words, using the trick Sarabeth had taught her about breaking big words into smaller ones.

She blamed concentrating on sounding out the words on the fact she didn't hear Dunne come down the stairs.

"What the hell do you think you're doing?"

She jumped and, much to her embarrassment, squeaked. When she whirled, she nearly toppled over at the pain vibrating through her leg.

Dunne's arm shot out, held her firmly so she didn't fall. But when she looked up at him, any relief she'd felt evaporated. Her mouth went to dust and her stomach dropped.

Well, she finally had a rise out of him.

But she suddenly didn't think that was such a great thing.

DUNNE HAD LEARNED a long time ago—long before he'd become a combat medic or gone to war—how to carefully wall off his emotions. When you were the grandson of an infamous serial killer, people were always looking for signs you had inherited the same kind of *bad* running through the blood.

So, he'd learned to give nothing, *nothing* away.

But there was a deep, hurting fury simmering inside of him and he was having a hell of a time leashing it back.

She'd had no right. He should have figured it out sooner. When she'd left his room without a scathing barb, he should have *known*.

"You don't let go of my arm pretty soon, you're gonna leave some bruises."

He dropped it like the soft skin of her arm had burned him. He didn't cause damage. He *healed*.

But for a blinding moment, he'd wanted to cause a little damage. Not to her specifically, just in general. He often wondered if he'd inherited that from his grandfather, those flashes of roughness, violence. Wondered if he was destined to unleash on the wrong person at the wrong time.

He stepped back, shoved his hands in his pockets, and still he knew he hadn't arranged his face into the appropriate stoicism.

"What's all this for?" she asked. "Like, why keep it a secret? You and your do-gooder brothers have to chase danger to feel alive, or whatever it is. Why so hush-hush?"

"Because it's none of your business, Quinn," he said. Carefully. Measuring each word.

And failing to keep the acid out of his tone.

She studied him with that frank brown gaze. She

lacked what he would call an awareness of social cues—and no wonder, she'd grown up off-the-grid, among a family of lunatics who'd been willing to kill and terrorize over the possibility of some old long-lost treasure. She'd been used as a pawn, traded and slid in and out of situations where she'd had to pretend to be her twin for years at a time.

It wasn't fair to hold that lack of understanding against her, but he didn't feel like being fair.

"Who's the Eye Socket Killer?"

Again, he couldn't school away his reaction. She'd said *socket* weird. With a long *e* sound. "Eye *socket*."

She shrugged. "Yeah, that's what I said."

He frowned. What did he care about how she pronounced certain words? But something about it, and the way she'd been using her finger to go over each word slowly, gave him an odd feeling. An itch.

She gave him too many damn itches.

"Again, none of your business," he said. Calmly this time. Maybe a hint of ice to his tone, but he'd pushed down the roiling anger inside him. He reached out to take her arm and lead her upstairs. "Now, why don't you go up—"

She stepped away from his grasp. "Like, unless it's you guys, which of course it's not. I've known killers. I've known psychopaths. You guys might be arrogant, steamrolling morons, but you're not psychotic murderers."

"Gee, thanks," he said dryly.

She grinned over her shoulder at him, which was one of those things that gave him an itch between his shoulder blades. It was a distraction, not ever a real sign of joy. Which made him wonder if she'd ever had anything to be happy about with her sad upbringing—which he didn't want to think about.

Because thinking about Quinn for too long never led anywhere good for him.

She was staring at the pictures, not horrified or disgusted. She studied them with an unaffected kind of interest. "Isn't it kind of weird that he kills men and women? Aren't serial killers supposed to pick one?"

Dunne said nothing. He wasn't going to have this conversation with her. In fact, he'd say nothing to her until she was upstairs. Let her poke around, ask her questions. He'd give her no information, no answers.

"This picture is labeled Idaho, but that ain't Idaho," she continued. "Trust me on that one."

"How can you tell?"

She pointed at the edge of a tree or a bush. "See this plant? It can't grow in the wild in Idaho. It could be cultivated to grow that big, but if this area is supposed to be isolated, it wouldn't be that big. It is supposed to be isolated, isn't it?"

"Thought you read the article?" he retorted, but he was studying the picture. A plant that wasn't supposed to be there. A mislabeled picture. Any of it could be a coincidence. But she'd noticed... "How'd you pick up on that? It's only a tiny part of a bush."

She shrugged. "I spent my life being forced to search for treasure no one even knew really existed. I'm pretty damn good at noticing patterns, oddities, and clues."

And that...changed things, didn't it? He could refuse

to engage, he could even shoo her upstairs, but she'd noticed something he and his brothers—who'd also been trained to look for clues and patterns—hadn't.

"What about the other pictures? Anything off on those?"

She stepped closer, pointed at the second one. "Where's it supposed to be?"

"It says right there," he said, pointing to the label.

She frowned. "Right. Yeah." She stared, frowning, but he got the impression she was looking at the word, not the picture. Her mouth moved a little, but no sound came out, like she was trying to sound out…

She couldn't read. Or at least, not well. He opened his mouth to say just that, but closed it at the look on her face. A sort of mutinous embarrassment that, surrounded by his own embarrassment, he didn't feel right poking at.

She'd grown up in a messed-up cult of sorts. Technically, she didn't even exist—no birth certificate, no identification. Landon was working on that for her, but she was still like a…lost woman.

Hardly her fault she couldn't read. She shouldn't be embarrassed about it, but he knew embarrassment didn't really follow rationale. Facts and feelings didn't always match up.

"This one's Louisiana," he said, pointing to the picture.

Her shoulders slumped. "I *can* read," she said defensively.

"Okay."

She straightened those shoulders and glared up at him. "I'm not stupid."

He held that angry gaze with a calm one of his own. "I never said you were."

For some reason, that only seemed to anger her more. She whirled away from the board and started stalking for the stairs.

He stopped her. Who knew why. He should let her go and hope she never came back down here.

But he stopped her, by standing in front of her and then when she tried to push passed him, by taking her arm in a gentle grip.

"Watch it. I'll—"

"What? Fake a punch, hit my injured leg instead? I've picked up on your pattern."

She grinned up at him. "I don't have a pattern."

It was only the slightest glimmer of morbid satisfaction in her eye that clued him in that he should angle his lower body away from her knee. Doing so narrowly saved him from a hit that definitely would have taken him to the ground.

He should have been irritated, but he only felt a kind of…pity for her. She really hadn't had a chance to be anything but combative and abrasive. But she'd escaped that life now. "It doesn't always have to be a fight, Quinn."

"Maybe in your world, Dunne. But not in mine."

Chapter Three

Quinn wasn't sure what was worse. That he thought she couldn't read—and was right—or that he *pitied* her.

Add on that he'd actually dodged her knee—even if only barely—she wanted to rage.

But she didn't. She was afraid if she let it all out, she'd end up crying. And she'd jump in front of a freight train before she cried in front of any of the Thompson brothers.

She thought about trying to hit him—leg, nose… whatever it took, but then she'd have to explain to Jessie why she'd beat up one of the guys who'd been so *kind* to her, and she'd end up feeling…guilty.

It was the worst part of this thing. Finding a sister, finding somewhere to be that wasn't being victim to her father's idiocy and insanity—she actually felt beholden. To Jessie. To Sarabeth.

And if she was really honest with herself, which she hated to be in the moment, Dunne. It was his combat medic training that had kept her from bleeding out so that she'd gotten to the hospital in time to be saved.

Hitting him wouldn't be right, and it was still a strange thing to have to worry about right and wrong.

"Would you let me go?" she said, attempting to sound bored rather than emotionally compromised.

"You noticed something none of us have," he said, back to all that calm. But even calm, he wasn't fully devoid of emotion now. This whole thing about serial killers had him worked up, even if he hid most of it away.

He let her go, his fingers slowly uncurling from her arm. It was an odd feeling. It sent a little tingling all the way up to the top of her head. She knew it was part attraction or chemistry or whatever—the Thompsons were a handsome lot. She liked flirting with them, even though none of them ever flirted back.

But there was something about the *intensity* of this feeling she didn't care for. So she went back to focusing on eyeless bodies.

"What do you care about all this? He kill someone you know or something?"

There was a flash—a *tiny*, *minuscule* flash of something—in his expression, but it was too quickly schooled away for her to identify what it was.

She wanted… She wanted to know what that flash was. What *this* was, and somehow that desire to know softened the words that came out of her mouth. "Tell me why," she said gently. When she wasn't sure she'd ever said anything gentle in her whole life.

Gentle got you killed. At best.

Dunne looked hard at his board. "There was a serial killer back in the fifties and sixties who used this MO."

"So, he's back?"

Dunne shook his head. "He died years ago. About a year after being sentenced to life in prison. It took police something like twenty-five years and fourteen known murders to track him down. This Eye Socket Killer is a copycat."

"Okay, but why do *you* care about either of them?" It had to be a victim thing. He knew one of the victims. He was avenging something, putting something to rights. That was *so* Thompson brothers. It explained the guilt, the need to fix something…that couldn't be fixed.

But, with his eyes on the board, Dunne shocked her. "The original Eye Socket Killer was my grandfather."

"Damn," Quinn said. Because, *wow*, that wasn't what she was expecting. "That's about as bad as my family. Maybe worse."

"Your sensitivity to the matter is astounding." His words were as dry as dust.

Quinn shrugged. Sensitivity definitely wasn't her strong suit. But his connection still didn't explain… "Unless you're going around eye-socketing people, what does your grandfather or his copycat have to do with you?"

"Eye-socketing." He blew out a gusty breath, and she almost—*almost*—thought it might be a laugh. Dunne's version of a laugh anyway. "It doesn't. Not really."

"But you've got all this."

"Yeah. I've got all this." He frowned at the board. "I don't have a good answer for that."

The words sounded like a lie, but she understood from the expression on his face—something far more tortured than his usual blank slate—that he didn't have a *good* answer or even one that made a lot of sense.

She'd been in a few complicated situations in her life to understand that feeling. The compulsion or need to do something, and the inability to fully explain why.

And because she had, and because maybe she'd finally found that chink in his armor she'd so desperately wanted to find—and now it just kind of made her sad or feel sorry for him—she figured she might as well help.

"I don't know much about Louisiana, but the plant was the clue in the picture that's supposed to be Idaho, so that's what I'd look into. The landscape in each of these photos. Does it match where they're supposedly from?"

His dark eyebrows drew together as he looked at the picture supposedly from Louisiana.

"What does it mean if they don't?"

"I don't know. It's just a step, right? When you're trying to solve a puzzle, you gather what you can for each step, and then see if it takes you to the next one."

He nodded thoughtfully. "Well, thanks for the tip."

Quinn laughed. "Oh, come on now. You know that's not the end of it. I'm in the club now."

He scowled. "What club?"

"The club where you and your brothers come down here, likely scour clues and toss theories back and forth. I want in. I *am* in."

He shook his head, which didn't surprise her in the least.

"I'm sure it's very manly, and the inclusion of someone with breasts would really put a damper on things, but I *did* figure out the picture thing, and there's more where that came from."

He didn't shake his head again, but he still looked 100 percent not interested. "Why?"

"I'm good at this kind of thing. What else am I going to do? I don't have ID or anything. I can't work. I've got this holding me back," she said, pointing at her leg.

This was the first…chance at something since she'd been shot. Something to *do*. Something to think about other than what the heck her future was going to be as a nearly thirty-year-old woman who could only barely read and didn't even *exist* on paper. "I've been working my whole life and now…*nothing*. I'm *bored*, Dunne. And I can help."

When he sorted through it later, Dunne figured it was the *bored* comment that really got to him. He knew it too well. When he'd been injured, he'd felt useless and bored and…well. It had taken a while to pull himself out of that pit.

Because he couldn't participate around the ranch at the same level his brothers did. He could patch people up, but when you were cowboys rather than soldiers, the need to heal didn't happen on a daily basis.

He'd been bored. Frustrated with his limitations and maybe, just maybe, that's why he'd started this whole thing in the first place. The chance to *do* something. Heal an old wound. Fixing something so many people were finding unfixable.

He didn't have to include her in everything, after all. Apparently she struggled to read—and no wonder with an upbringing like hers—but it would keep her from delving too deeply into the whole thing. She could look at pictures and feel like she was offering something.

She *had* offered something. The pictures of the bodies not matching the locations reported. It was an interesting pattern. One he struggled not to obsess over.

It might be easy to rule out a location, but it was going to be a lot harder to figure out the actual place. And where that breakdown occurred. With the photographer? The reporter? Law enforcement? Something deeper and more sinister than all that?

Over the next few days, he tried to focus on the ranch, on Quinn's physical therapy. On *life* rather than death. He didn't let himself go to the basement. He needed balance, and he had *excellent* self-control.

Or so he told himself.

Quinn didn't bring it up either when they worked on their physical therapy, but she also didn't poke at him like she usually did. No digs about *his* leg, no flashes of outrageous flirtation he knew were meant to make him feel uncomfortable and back off—not *actual* flirtation.

One night, sitting around the dinner table, shoved together because there were far too many people in this house trying to eat at the same table, Dunne knew the moment Cal walked in, he had something to tell him.

When he said nothing in front of everyone, Dunne figured it was another lead in the case. But he wouldn't bring it up until they were alone—or at least until Sarabeth was out of the vicinity.

Dunne hadn't asked his brothers to keep this a secret

from their significant others. It wasn't so much that it was a secret. It was just that…

Hell, he didn't know. He didn't want to have conversations around the dining room table about serial killers and eye sockets and his *grandfather*. If they played it like this, he could compartmentalize the whole thing. Set it aside when it needed setting aside.

Study what he had in the designated hours he had for research and investigation.

It had been Kate's turn to make dinner, so it was particularly delicious as she was by far the best cook, but Dunne didn't taste it. He thought about what the new lead could be.

A clue? Another victim? Someone he hadn't been able to save?

When he caught Quinn studying him, he stood from the table. No one questioned his early exit. He'd cleaned his plate and it wasn't his turn to do dishes. So he deposited his plate and went to his room.

Cal would find him. Tell him what was up. Then they'd deal with it. Study, investigate.

Come up empty.

Dunne pushed that thought away. Getting frustrated and maudlin didn't solve a difficult problem. Patience and stoicism did. Dedication and the refusal to give up. But also the refusal to let something take over your entire life.

Like this wanted to.

Dunne busied himself by cleaning up his room until it was military precision. Bed made. Supplies put away.

When an hour had passed and Cal still hadn't come to find him, Dunne went back to the kitchen.

Cal was helping Jessie finish up the dishes while Sarabeth yammered on from the porch, her voice carrying through the screen. Likely she was playing with her cat.

Eventually, she came inside, and Cal told Jessie he could handle the rest of cleanup, and the two disappeared.

Once it was just him and Cal, Cal nodded, washing down the kitchen counter.

"Another body is being reported found. This time in Kansas," Cal said, his voice low. He jutted his chin toward the basement door as he tossed the washcloth into the dirty pile.

Dunne nodded, and Cal opened the door and went downstairs. Dunne was about to follow when someone cleared their throat.

He looked back to find Quinn standing behind the screen door. She gave him one little eyebrow raise. She'd been eavesdropping, he had no doubt. He should tell her to go to hell. No, he should just ignore her.

But what was one more set of eyes?

He winced a little at the thought of *eyes* in this context, but he waved her downstairs anyway.

She followed him, and he didn't miss the little hiss of breath she let out at the first step. He'd been there too. The frustration, the pain, the useless feeling.

Cal said nothing when they got to the basement. His expression gave away nothing. And still Dunne had no doubt Cal disapproved.

But he didn't argue. He waited for Dunne's nod, then started.

"Body in Kansas. Eyes removed. Didn't have a chance to print out the article, but here it is." He handed Dunne his phone.

Dunne skimmed it. Nothing jumped out at him as a major clue. MO was the same. Cops had no leads per usual. Everything was the *same*. Only the places ever changed.

Frustrating, but he couldn't show it. He walked stiffly over to the board and wrote "KS" on his list of states the murders occurred in. He'd been trying to find a geographic pattern to the murders. Some sort of map to where the killer might hit next, but it seemed so random.

"Maybe it's the letters," Quinn suggested, speaking for the first time.

"Letters?" Cal returned with thinly veiled suspicion.

"These letters," Quinn said, pointing to the state abbreviations he had listed, and just added "KS" to.

"W-Y, I-D, L-A and now K-S," Quinn said out loud. "Maybe it spells something?"

Dunne felt cold all over. It didn't spell anything, as far as he knew. But all the letters to his real last name were right there, the KS from Kansas tying it all up in a bow.

Wilks.

Coincidence. Surely. There were letters leftover. It was just...a weird, uncomfortable coincidence.

But he glanced at Cal and saw the same kind of uneasiness on his face, because Cal knew his real last name too.

"But you said that one picture isn't Idaho," Dunne pointed out, wanting—maybe needing—for this not to actually be some kind of clue. Because his grandfather was his mother's father, which meant Dunne didn't share a last name with him. So this was no connection to his grandfather.

It was to him.

"No, it isn't Idaho, but the article said it was, right? So…even if it's not, someone wants people to think it is. Maybe the real states or cities or something spell out something else."

"I guess that means we need to figure out where these pictures were really taken," Cal offered.

"And who reported the bodies were somewhere they weren't," Quinn pointed out. "There's a breakdown somewhere. The cops? Before the cops? Reporters? Photographers? Someone knows more in this chain of information."

And it was time for Dunne to figure out who that was. Even if it meant leaving the ranch and finally getting to the bottom of things.

Once and for all.

Chapter Four

Quinn studied the pictures, but she hadn't traveled much outside of the wilderness in Idaho, Montana and Wyoming. A little inland Washington and northern Colorado, here and there.

"Maybe Landon can run them through some kind of computer-imaging program," Cal suggested. "I'll send out some emails to the reporters and photographers, see if we get a bite."

"We don't want to tip him off," Dunne said very carefully. And not in his normal careful way, but more weighty. Something was different about him since she'd pointed out the letters.

"No, we don't, but we need more information to go on. I'll be careful."

Dunne nodded, but his gaze hadn't left the board. The list of state abbreviations specifically.

What pattern did he see there? Something. Something enough to shake him—in that tiny, minuscule way. Something around his mouth, or the intensity of his gaze.

But what if underneath that tiny blip of emotions was the stronger, more volatile ones like she'd seen bubbling inside of him when he'd found her down here without permission?

An interesting—far too interesting—thought.

"I'll go see what Landon's up to," Cal said.

Dunne nodded, but didn't head for the stairs like Cal did, so Quinn stayed put as well. Cal took the first step, then turned around as if he realized they hadn't followed.

"Are you two just staying down here? Together?" Cal asked, one eyebrow raised.

She didn't like the odd…incredulousness to Cal's expression, like he thought something untoward was going on but also like he couldn't *believe* something could ever possibly happen between her and Dunne.

"Yeah, I thought I'd jump him in front of the most morbid bulletin board that's ever existed. Oh, baby." She reached out and trailed her fingertips down Dunne's arm.

Dunne scowled and stepped away from her.

Cal sighed, a long-suffering one, which was the only way he seemed to know how to sigh. He muttered to himself as he disappeared upstairs.

Quinn grinned at Dunne, but he wasn't looking at her. He was looking at the letters. Clearly he saw something in them.

"What do those letters mean to you?" she asked. She'd gotten this far by just asking, after all.

He looked up at them, one of those long pauses she thought meant more than him just thinking things through.

"Nothing, really."

"Liar."

He turned to glare at her. "You don't know me, Quinn. Trust me, you don't know when I'm lying."

"I've got a pretty good BS detector. Knowing you or not doesn't matter. I watch, I observe, I figure it out. Those letters meant something to you."

He shrugged. "Just all states I've been to, and the original Eye Socket Killer killed in Louisiana and Kansas. Maybe the other states too. That's the problem with serial killers, you can never be sure you've found all their victims."

"Cheering thought."

"Nothing about this is all that cheerful," he replied in his usual calm, detached flatness.

But he was not detached from this whole thing. He was standing there staring at those letters like they might jump out and scream 'Hello, my name is Murderer Guy, arrest me.'

"When did it start?"

"What? The murders?"

"The copycat murders," Quinn clarified.

"A year ago."

"Sure. But like, when?"

He shrugged, but there was something in that shrug. In that *movement* over stillness. She was homing in on something he hadn't considered, and he didn't like it. But he wanted all the answers.

"We only have the information reported by police or by journalists. If those pictures are wrong, then any information can be wrong."

"Sure, but it's still information. It's still something."

She went over and pointed to the board where the number *1* was. Information on the first murder, she assumed. "When was this one?"

He opened his mouth, and if she wanted to hazard a guess, he was about to make a crack about her reading it herself. She could see it in the way he wanted to snap, then carefully closed his mouth. Carefully adopted all that *blank*. No, making a crack about her reading skills or lack thereof wasn't his style. Too good, too *noble*.

Usually, she'd bristle at that, but she knew she was on to something with the dates, and she found the prospect of unraveling a mystery too exciting—*finally* something to do, to think about, to maybe feel useful over. "When, Dunne?"

He made a face. An actual *expression* that was all frustration. "It's unclear, but the first *found* murder has been narrowed down to sometime between January 12 and January 15 of last year."

"Does either date mean anything to you?"

He was very quiet, very still. It *did* mean something. Clearly.

"Clearly I'm offering you some patterns you didn't see or notice before—and neither did any of your brothers. Points for me."

"This isn't a game."

Quinn rolled her eyes. "It's also got nothing to do with you. Allegedly. It's not even your actual *grandpa* doing these current murders."

"It's someone copying him," Dunne returned. So stubborn she was tempted to reach out and shake him. Only the way he kept his eyes fixed on those letters kept her from actually doing it. Because there was something *haunted* in the dark green depths. A *haunted* she understood far better than she wanted to.

"There's something that connects you. In those letters. In that date."

He said nothing. He didn't move. But his eyes slowly shifted to look at her with irritation and suspicion.

"You can fool your brothers, I think, because you know them so well. But you don't know me, so you can't fool me."

"That's illogical."

"Not at all. You know them well enough to know how to put up the right walls they don't know how to look behind. You know how to say the right things so they won't poke into what you don't want them to poke into. You have the most control. The one with the best poker face—probably from all that medic stuff you had to do. They're arrogant enough to think they can see when you're lying to them, because they all have little tells. But you don't. Not very often."

"Then how can you, someone who doesn't know me, see through me?"

"Because you don't know how to fool me. And because I may not have grown up with schools and military training or real family devotion or whatever, but I grew up with a bunch of men I had to learn to understand if I wanted to survive. I know how to pick people apart. Even the stoic ones."

And she knew enough to see she wouldn't get the information out of him. Not yet. But that didn't mean she wouldn't. And it didn't mean she couldn't keep poking at other pieces of this whole mystery. "So, what do you plan to do next?"

He shrugged. "Same as I have been."

Quinn considered it luck in this moment that she'd grown up surrounded by men, because she knew exactly what was going on in Dunne's mind.

He wanted to *act*. Partly because he was frustrated with putting the pieces of this mystery together, and partly because something about those letters had scared him.

When men like the ones she'd been raised around got scared, they blamed other people. Ranted and raved. They took it out with fists and weapons.

Quinn tried to think about what a good man would do instead. If a bad man's thought process was to hurt, the opposite of that would be to…protect.

"Do you think your brothers will buy that?"

His eyebrows drew together infinitesimally. "Huh?"

"Anyone with half a brain can tell you're planning to go after the killer. And you think you're going to leave everyone behind. So my question is do you really think you can con your brothers? I know you can freeze them out, but can you straight up deceive them?"

His expression took on the faintest sheen of ice then. Not just cool detachment, but cold, targeted anger. "It's not deceit."

"It will be, if you leave without telling them what you're up to. That's the plan, isn't it?"

He turned to her then, just the hint of temper in the movement. But he kept his voice flat, even as he jabbed his thumb into his own chest. "This is *my* deal."

Quinn clucked her tongue and shook her head. "Not this time, cowboy. I'm in, and you can try to shake me, but you don't stand a chance."

DUNNE RARELY FOUND himself at a loss for words. He was often silent, often kept words to himself, but he always *had* the words, even if he didn't utter them.

Quinn made no sense. She all but ran circles around him. With the letters, with the dates, with the whole seeing-through-him thing.

And she was right, unfortunately, about all of it. That he knew more. That he was going to deceive his brothers. That he could put up a shield between him and them that they never fully saw.

Where had she come from? What the hell was he supposed to do with her?

"I'm sure two debilitated people can hunt down a mass murderer," he said with as much biting sarcasm as he could manage. God knew she spoke fluent sarcasm, knew how to use it like a weapon. Maybe that was the only way to get rid of her.

"But one could?" She made a scoffing noise. "Come on, Dunne. Two is better than one. You don't want your brothers tagging along because, well, for starters, you care about what happens to them but also because they've got a ranch to run and everyone but Cal has someone to tend or be tended by. But I'm like you. I've got nothing to do, nothing to offer the ranch—or very little anyway. So, we'll do it together."

Her easy estimation of what he was to this ranch… hurt. When it shouldn't. The truth should never hurt.

He couldn't offer the same kind of physical labor his brothers could. Oh sure, he could keep the books, or do some basic chores. If something required upper body strength, he could be counted on.

But his leg made horse riding difficult. Anything that required too much walking or too many quick maneuvers put undue stress on his bad leg. He knew he had a place on this ranch, and that he wasn't completely useless.

But he also knew that…he was easily replaceable. Aside from the whole medical-training thing—which usually only came in handy when his brothers were getting themselves involved in things they shouldn't— Kate or Jessie could easily step in and do what he did.

And she saw it. In just a few weeks of being here, Quinn could break it down into the simple truth.

Just like she'd made sense of the state abbreviations spelling something—even if she didn't know what. Just like pointing out the date of the first murder meant something.

He'd already considered that but could dismiss it as coincidence. Just because the first reported murder happened in the same time frame as his birthday didn't have to mean anything.

But the letters spelling out his last name added another layer to that. With just enough wrong—extra letters—to make him wonder if he was crazy. Hyperfocusing on himself when this had nothing to do with him.

But it sure felt like it had something to do with him.

"So, when do we leave?" Quinn asked, cheerfully almost. Like it was a done deal.

He crossed his arms over his chest, looked down at her and worked up his best military commanding officer voice. "Do you honestly think I'm going to let you come with me?"

"Oh, I'm coming with you. No *letting* necessary. You can choose the hard way, or the easy way, but I'll be there."

"I don't want you there."

She shrugged. "Tough, babe."

It was the *babe* that snapped his famed control. He stepped close to her, towered over her really—and that was the point. To show her he could be physically intimidating if he wanted to be. "I wouldn't test me, Quinn."

She laughed. In his face. "Yeah, you're real scary with that obvious, shining beacon of honor."

"You have no idea what I've done." He'd been a soldier. He'd been to war. He'd killed as much as he'd saved some days.

But she didn't wilt. If anything, the set of her jaw hardened as did her dark eyes. "And you have no idea what's been done to me."

He took a step back. Point taken. She'd won that round, he'd give her that.

But like hell she was coming with him. Still, telling her no wasn't the way forward. "I need to gather a little more intel first. I wouldn't leave this week. Maybe next. It has to be the right moment, and I have to make sure however I leave, my brothers won't follow."

She nodded thoughtfully. "Makes sense. Probably best to figure out where those pictures were really taken first. Then you either go to the first murder or the most recent. Which would you choose?"

He wanted to tell her neither, but of course first or most recent was the most reasonable question. "Depends."

"No, it doesn't. To solve a pattern, you start at the beginning."

"Why are you asking if you've got such strong opinions?"

She shrugged. "It's your deal. I'm just in it to feel useful and because I'll be more help than the five of your brothers combined—no offense to them. You can run the show. I'm just going to tell you when you're wrong."

"It's not right or wrong. It's a matter of opinion." Of course, she was right. As things stood now, if they could find the actual location of the first murder, the most sensible first step would be to go there.

But he wasn't about to admit that to her. She had too big of a head already.

"I'm sure my brothers and I would have figured out the letters thing soon enough."

"I'll give you that, but not the pictures. None of you know Idaho enough to pick out that picture wasn't Idaho. Doubtful for the other states either. Where are you guys from, anyway? None of your accents match."

"I don't have an accent."

"Everyone has an accent. Landon's southern. Mississippi, if I had to guess. Jake's is easy. Pennsylvania, probably Pittsburgh. Brody's Chicago, through and through. Henry is Midwestern, too, but more northern. I'd guess Michigan. Cal is tough, but not impossible. East Coast, but inland. There's a hint of that Southern accent. Maryland maybe. Could be northern Virginia. He suppresses it a little, but he's got nothing on you. You're the hardest, because you don't speak much. You've got a combo in there. Maybe a decent chunk of time in Maine or Vermont. But based on your choice of profession pre-cowboy days, I'd lay money on military brat." She turned to face him with a questioning frown. "How are you brothers if you grew up in such different places?"

He tried not to let it show how much she'd rattled him. She'd been spot-on. For each and every one of them. "You, who just met your twin sister at what? Thirty? You're asking me how they can be my brothers?"

"I'm twenty-nine, thank you very much. I also look exactly like my sister."

"Not exactly."

"Oh really? Name *one* difference."

He pointed to his earlobe. "Jessie has a freckle right here. You don't."

"I can't decide which one of us you've been staring inappropriately at."

It took him more self-control than usual not to react to that. She was trying to bait him, not accusing him of anything. He had no earthly reason to feel guilty or *inappropriate*. He was an observer, and anyone who lived with near-identical twins had to spend some time determining what you could use to tell them apart.

It wasn't just the freckle, of course. It was in how they talked, how they held themselves. It was down to how they *moved*, but he wasn't about to tell her that.

When the silence of his reaction spread out, she finally sighed.

"You're avoiding my questions, but we can let it lie."

"Gee, thanks."

She shrugged. "Point is, none of you know the West like I do. I could pick that out. I can pick a lot of things out. Twenty-nine of those years I was raised, bred and fed on following patterns and unraveling mysteries with a lot less to go on. Murder—that's something to go on."

It was clear there was no point in arguing with her. She would only dig her heels in further. He needed to nod, agree and let her think she was in on it. Then he'd shake her off, just like he'd shake his brothers off, and he'd take care of this.

And whoever wanted to tangle him in his grandfather's old murders. Because his name and his birthdate meant this *was* about him. Somehow. Someway.

"I don't suppose I could take one of those binders to my room? I'm not exactly a quick reader."

His knee-jerk was to refuse. She didn't need to be reading his binders. She didn't need to do anything.

But she wanted to, and even if it wasn't a full admission, she was showing a little weakness by admitting she didn't read quickly. "Sure."

"Thanks."

She grabbed the binder that was about the first murder. The exact one he'd wanted to study this evening.

He didn't say anything though, and he didn't scowl. He just let her head toward the stairs, binder under her arm, while he stayed where he was.

"Oh, and Dunne?" She turned on the stairs, the solitary light bulb creating a halo behind her that tinged her dark hair red, made her look…

Well, it didn't do him any good to consider how she looked.

"Try and leave without me." She smiled sweetly and batted her eyelashes at him. "I *dare* you."

Chapter Five

Quinn hadn't felt this good in *months*. Maybe it was twisted—she wasn't afraid to admit she might be twisted—but having something to concentrate on, to figure out… Well, it was a hell of a lot better than lying around, wallowing in her pain and wondering what on earth she was going to do with the rest of her life.

Besides, if nothing else, she figured going through the binder was good reading practice. Frustrating, since a lot of the words were way above her skill level. But she struggled through as many articles as she could that night, and then the next, all while watching Dunne closely for signs he was getting ready to bolt.

She knew he'd try to leave without her. *Knew* it. Even as she sat on the porch and watched him talk to Landon in front of the rebuilt stables, looking like he was relaxed and involved.

She knew. Inside, he was wound tight. Wired.

She hadn't figured out what his connection was yet—the real connection he wasn't letting anyone in on—but she would.

"You've been paying an awful lot of attention to Dunne."

Quinn blinked and looked up at her sister, who'd come out to join her on the porch without Quinn realizing it.

"Huh?"

Jessie nodded toward Dunne and Landon. "Sure, they're both nice to look at, but you have been zeroed in on Dunne for days."

Quinn looked at her sister, and then realized what Jessie was tactfully trying to get at. "You're worried I have a *crush* on him?" That was ridiculous. She wasn't a teenage girl.

"That probably isn't the word I'd use. More like… an *interest*."

"Better, but still not true." Well, in the way Jessie meant. Mostly. Sure, he was hot. All the Thompson brothers were, varying accents or not.

But her interest was of the puzzle sort. Nothing else.

Because she knew what she was.There was no hope for being a normal woman. Not with nearly thirty years of messed up under her belt.

Jessie sat down in another one of the porch chairs. Quinn could tell she wanted to say more, but she was weighing the words first. Which meant it was serious. Which meant Quinn wanted to cut this off at the pass.

"Trust me, sis, I've learned how to look, appreciate and steer *way* clear."

But that didn't make Jessie laugh or seem to change the subject. She looked as serious as ever.

"Men aren't all bad."

Quinn tried not to fidget under the steady gaze of her sister. They hadn't grown up together, but Quinn had grown up knowing she had an identical twin out there. Jessie hadn't.

But even knowing it hadn't fully prepared her for just sitting here talking to someone who looked like Quinn was sitting in front of a mirror.

As for men being bad? Well, it was hard to argue when she was in the midst of all that Thompson hard-headed nobleness.

"No, you found yourself a passel of good ones."

"You've found them too," Jessie said, still so dang serious. "I want to make sure you know that. That you understand that. No matter what happens, what choices you make, you have a home with me. You belong. And right now, my home is here. So you're not a temporary guest. Unless you want to be."

This time Quinn did fidget in her chair. She angled herself a little away from Jessie and squinted into the late evening sun. She swallowed at the painful lump in her throat and blinked hard. *You belong.* She'd never had a home, not really. She'd never belonged, because she'd been raised a pawn.

She didn't belong here. Jessie did. Jessie hadn't done anything wrong in her life. She had a cute kid. Henry was gone over the both of them. Jessie had a family, a life. At best, Quinn was some kind of…baggage.

But she didn't have anywhere else to go yet.

"Quinn, I'm serious," Jessie said, reaching across and giving Quinn's shoulder a squeeze.

Quinn forced her mouth to curve. "Yeah, sure. Thanks."

Jessie sighed, likely because she understood Quinn was just agreeing to move on, not because she believed it. "We're family. You, me and Sarabeth. No matter how far apart we were raised. You're my twin sister. We're family."

"Being part of the Peterson family has never been much of a boon, Jessie." She'd meant to say it with a grin, a joke. But it was all bitterness. A heavy weight of what being born into that family had meant.

"It will be. We'll make it a boon. From here on out."

Since it was a nice thought, that she and Jessie and Sarabeth could create some kind of good family out of all the bad they'd been dealt, Quinn smiled for real now. Maybe this was never going to be her home, and maybe she'd never belong anywhere, but Jessie was her sister and Sarabeth was her niece.

That would always mean something more than anything she'd had before.

"So, if I set my sights on one of them, who would I break first? Cal or Dunne?"

Jessie laughed, shading her eyes against the setting sun to look out at where the six brothers had gathered. Then she laughed again. "Normally I'd say no one could break either of them, but I think you could break anyone you set your sights on breaking."

Dunne either heard Jessie laughing or sensed that they were talking about him. He turned and his gaze met Quinn's across the yard. That dark, mysterious green. The flat line of his mouth. The sun hitting him in such a way he very nearly seemed to glow, reminding her of some kind of Greek god statue or something.

And she recognized some of what swept through her—basic attraction, sure. But there was this little… flutter in the center of her chest she didn't understand or like at all.

She wasn't the fluttering sort. She wasn't like Jessie. She didn't have white picket fence dreams. She just wanted the chance to…live her own life. That was all.

No muscled, scowling, frustrating male complications. No way.

Just a mystery to solve.

Her specialty.

DUNNE SURVEYED HIS GEAR. It wasn't much. He'd culled and culled and culled some more. It wasn't going to be easy to sneak out of the house, even in the middle of the night. His brothers were trained to wake and be ready for any possible disruption at any time.

Luckily, love had softened the majority of them. Everyone but Cal was likely all cozied up with their significant other, instincts dulled by *happiness* and satisfaction.

Now that Dunne had the information he needed, he'd planned it out. Where to go, what to carry, and how to avoid alerting anyone to his movements. Until there was nothing they could do to stop him.

Landon had found the real locations of three of the photographs, and the abbreviations clarified everything Dunne worried was true.

Delaware. Utah. North Dakota.

D-U-N. Which meant, if the pattern followed, the last picture—which depicted the first murder—was Nebraska.

The fake locations spelled out his last name. The real locations spelled out his first name.

If his brothers had noticed that pattern, they'd kept it to themselves. Or they were waiting for the Nebraska confirmation.

Dunne didn't need it. These states spelled out his name. First and last. There was no blaming things on coincidence anymore.

This connected to him. He didn't understand why or how. But it did. His old life. Before the military. Before his brothers.

So, this was his mission and his mission alone.

He'd start in Nebraska—it was the first murder's actual location, assuming that the first murder reported was the *first*.

Based on the name, the birthdate connection, he had a bad feeling it was. Then he would set out to track down a murderer. It wasn't all that different than what he'd done in the military.

He knew it put him in some jeopardy. Technically, Dunne Wilks was supposed to be dead. If the few military higher-ups who knew about him found out he was trailing after murderers anywhere outside of Wilde, Wyoming, he might face a lot of potential problems. Being forced off the ranch and away from his brothers, at best.

But he had to do this, and for that reason alone, he knew he could keep his brothers at bay. They all had good reason to stay on the ranch, off the radar of the military brass. They had no good reason to risk their futures here. Even Cal wouldn't want to risk losing what they'd built. Cal wouldn't admit it to himself, but he'd settled into the ranch, unclenched a little bit.

They'd stay. And Dunne would come back. Once he finished this mission.

As long as he didn't get caught, or land too much on anyone's radar.

Luckily, he was the only one whose room was on the first floor. It'd be easier to sneak out the back or even the side, but both entrances were in clear view of the little outbuilding Brody and Kate occupied.

So it was out the front. He'd tested this route. How to avoid the squeaks in the floorboard, how to open the door just so, without it making a noise. Waiting for the cat to inevitably come bounding down the stairs in her typical late-night antics to cover the sounds of him closing the door behind him.

Anything anyone might hear, they'd chalk up to Henrietta.

He moved quickly off the porch and to his truck. He'd parked it so that taking off the brake would allow enough momentum to keep the vehicle in neutral and get him to the road. Maybe even down it a ways. Enough.

He moved silently and quickly through the heavy dark of midnight. Before he reached his truck, he stopped abruptly. There wasn't a sound, just the subtle movement in shadow. It could be a trick of the late evening dark, it could be an animal, but...

He reached out, unerringly came up with someone. Not one of his brothers. The kick to the shin surprised him but didn't take him down. He kept his grip on the person's arm, twisted.

He could have told Quinn he knew it was her, even in the dark. He could smell her, feel the strength in her arm that wasn't the same as any of his brothers.

He could have told her a fight was not what her injured leg needed, but instead, he dodged her attempt to kick him again. She tried to get an elbow to his gut, but she didn't have enough leverage and it just bounced off.

He managed to get her other arm, holding her tightly enough and close enough she was mostly immobile.

"You're going to have to fight without relying on that bum leg," he informed her, his voice quiet and close to her ear.

"Well, I suppose you could teach me," she said, not winded. Not even acting scared or angry. Just offhanded. As though nothing ever bothered her.

She really was exhausting, even if he begrudgingly admired her determination. "I could teach you. Doesn't mean I will." He would have held her there, afraid of what she might do, except she'd gone still. Relaxed.

It became something less like a fighter's hold and more like an embrace.

He dropped his hands.

"You'll teach me," she said, her voice quiet but cheerful enough. "The way I see it, we've got nothing but time ahead of us. Where we headed? The first one was Wyoming, right? But not Wyoming. So, where was it really?"

He scowled. But he couldn't hold it. She was tireless. And because he didn't know her that well, he didn't know how to shake her. Unfortunately, time was of the essence. He couldn't waste it standing here arguing with her or trying to figure a way to send her back to the house.

At best, he had about five minutes before one of his brothers woke up and caught on. He had to leave and at this point, she knew too much.

So, he sighed. "It was Nebraska."

She trailed after him as he headed for his truck. "Nebraska. N-E. Did you figure out where the other ones really happened?"

There was telling her some things and telling her everything, but she tossed a bag into the truck just as he did. She had nothing to lose, he supposed, as long as he kept her out of any potential danger. Maybe it wasn't such a bad thing to have another set of eyes—ones that knew how to unravel a mystery pretty damn quick.

He didn't *like* the idea, but in the moment, getting away from the house before one of his brothers sensed something was off trumped liking anything.

"Nebraska, North Dakota, Utah and Delaware."

"That spells your name," she pointed out, oh-so helpfully as they both climbed into the truck, and carefully closed their doors without slamming them.

He didn't know why he was going with the pretense, but it was like an ingrained habit. "No, N-E, N-D, U-T, D-E spells nothing." He released the brake, shifted the truck into neutral, and they began their slow roll descent to the road.

"But the D in D-E, the U in U-T, the N in N-D, and then the N and E in N-E. D-U-N-N-E," Quinn said. "Reading might not be my strong suit, but I know how to spell your name. The other ones, the fake locations, did they spell something? Not *Thompson*. What did they spell?"

He didn't have to tell her. He was pretty good at not telling people things. And there was no way she'd figure it out on her own. To come up with his last name would require...

"Well, if it's in order, like the first name, the fake states are Wyoming, Idaho, Louisiana and Kansas. But Dunne was backwards. Nebraska the first real murder, then so on. First four first letters. Last one, both letters, then backwards. The real locations don't spell anything in backwards order, but maybe this one is just forwards. So... *Wilks*?"

Damn, she was sharp. Figured he'd be stuck with a woman who'd spent her entire life looking for patterns and clues.

"Yeah."

"What's that mean to you? Your grandpa's name? His kid?"

Dunne shook his head. "My maternal grandfather. His name was Earl Dunne."

"So it could connect to him, rather than you, since your name is also his last name," she pondered.

He could feel her gaze on him as he turned the ignition. Not as far from the house as he'd like, but he was losing momentum in neutral.

"But you don't think it connects to your grandfather. You think it connects to you."

Dunne sighed. She was here. She knew too much and figured out things quicker than he did—which grated as much as it might help. She might as well know. In the end, weirdly, it was better than one of his brothers. She risked nothing by being here, and he'd keep her safe no matter what.

It wasn't the worst-case scenario, even if something inside of him felt dread at the prospect.

"Wilks is my real last name. So, maybe it connects to my grandfather too, but it connects to me. One hundred percent."

Quinn made a thoughtful noise. "So it's a family thing. And your brothers aren't your family."

"Yes, they are."

He could sense the eye roll more than he could see it. "Not biologically, I mean. The accent thing, the looks thing—you're just pretending to be biological brothers."

"Yes."

"Why?"

"Here's the deal. I've let you tag along because you risk nothing and I couldn't risk wasting time."

"And because I'm better at puzzles than you."

He wanted to argue. She wasn't *better*. He even opened his mouth to do so, but that didn't matter. Let her think she was better.

"But there are rules. I'm in charge. You don't follow my rules, you're gone," he said, ignoring her comment about *better*. "Number one is, you let the subject of my brothers go."

She studied him in the way she had that made him wonder how he measured up in her estimation. When he always knew how people measured him.

"I'm serious. You will do what I say. You will not argue. You will stay put when I tell you to. That's the only way I'm actually letting you come with me."

She shrugged. "If you say so." The kind of easy that was never real agreement.

He could belabor the point, he supposed. But it wasn't his style. He'd rather spend the nighttime drive to Nebraska in utter silence.

Quinn clearly felt differently. "You need me. Not just because of the puzzles thing, but because you'll be less conspicuous with a woman traveling with you. One big, muscled, limping man with absolutely no charm whatsoever sticks out."

"But two limping people with no charm whatsoever blends in?"

She grinned at him in the dim light of the truck's interior. "I can be charming, Dunne. I can be just about anything."

Dread slithered through him. Not at what she'd said, but at the very irritating reaction his body had to that smile and those words.

He was in trouble. And for once in his life, he didn't know how to get out of it.

Chapter Six

Quinn blinked her eyes open and groaned at the ache in her neck. She'd fallen asleep with it at a painful angle and now she was paying the price. She tried to work out the kinks as she looked around.

Daylight, dim and misty, surrounding a rather bustling gas station. Dunne wasn't in the driver's seat. He was likely inside.

Smart to pick somewhere busy where they wouldn't really be noticed. Just a road-tripping couple stopping along the way for gas. Her stomach rumbled. Hopefully snacks too.

She continued to look around, wondering if she should get out or if they should take turns with that kind of thing. One person always keeping kind of on the down low.

She didn't know exactly what Dunne was hiding from. Was he just trying to protect his brothers, who would likely want to come after him? Or was he worried about something else?

She might be able to unravel this mystery stuff easily enough, but she still hadn't unraveled Dunne or why he and his brothers pretended to be related when they weren't really.

She would, but she thought she could be patient on that score. Maybe. Long as this whole serial killer thing remained interesting.

The door to the convenience store opened and Dunne appeared carrying a variety of items. Quinn's stomach rumbled again. But something else fluttered there along with hunger.

He wore the cowboy hat like he'd been born in one, but she wondered how many people could read the military on him. The Thompson brothers all had it. A kind of watchfulness. Like they weren't quite certain they were ever safe, even if they knew they were capable of dealing with whatever threat presented itself.

She watched a woman waiting for her car to gas up follow Dunne with her eyes. *She* definitely saw something she liked—cowboy, military or other. Quinn couldn't blame her for that.

Dunne opened the driver's-side door and slid into his chair. He handed her a few snack items he'd been carrying in the crook of his arm. "Didn't know what you liked, so take your pick."

She grabbed the closest and shrugged. "I'll eat anything."

He eyed her as if he read a million things in that one simple statement, and she supposed he had enough background to make those kinds of assumptions.

She shouldn't care, and in a *way* she didn't. But she didn't want any sort of…pity. Not from him. "You know, it's not so bad."

"What isn't?"

"Growing up in some kind of weird cult, compound thing. At least the one I was in. Sure, it sucked, but I can think of a lot worse."

"Just because you can think of worse doesn't make what you went through okay."

That simple statement had something twisting deep inside of her chest that she wanted absolutely *nothing* to do with. "I didn't *go* through it. It just happened. It just was. I survived."

"I'm not talking about survival."

The twisting feeling turned into something more akin to clawing. Painful. She shoved a handful of pretzels into her mouth so she didn't end up saying something bad-tempered and nasty. Only because bad-tempered and nasty would probably prove whatever dumb point he was trying to make.

He pulled out of the parking lot of the gas station, heading toward the sun rising in the east. "This Nebraska?" she asked through a mouthful of pretzels.

The gaze he slid her was too calculated and too soft at the same time. Like he could see all the trauma marked on her skin, when she was *fine*. She'd survived and gotten out and what was sad about that?

That she couldn't read all that well? She was learning. That she didn't have a family? Jessie had promised to be there, no matter what, and Quinn had proven she'd do whatever it took to save Jessie and Sarabeth.

So, no, there was nothing to *pity* her over.

"Yeah, we crossed the state line. About another hour

till we get to Springview. That'll be a good place to stay and work from."

"How are we going to uncover things without your murder board?"

His sigh was long-suffering, which eased over some of the spiky feelings inside of her. Annoying him really was a balm. "I've got the information I need."

She had no doubt he did. For the time being anyway. And why not hop right into some of the things she'd been pondering when it got her mind off her own stuff? "Have you considered that all the clues connecting to you are meant to prompt you into coming after him?"

"It's safe to assume I've considered everything. That. Being framed. A million scenarios I can't even fathom because it takes someone with a completely unreasonable mind to murder this many people, all while leaving *clues*. So, considered? Sure. I have to consider everything."

"I doubt you've considered everything. Like you said, serial killers don't lean toward the sane or reasonable."

"Your constant reassurance makes me so glad I let you browbeat me into accompanying me."

"I didn't have to browbeat. I just had to show up. You gave up real easy. I thought I'd have to really fight you."

"You kicked my shin."

She laughed, couldn't help it. "I've done worse. To you."

He scowled but didn't argue anymore. He focused on the road and his driving. His expression slowly went grave, like he was thinking things over and not liking what he came up with.

"It connects to my family in some way. The names. The dates. It isn't just coincidence."

"No, it isn't," Quinn agreed, feeling the tiniest bit sorry for him. It seemed to really bother him that this connected to his family. She couldn't really access why that might be hard for him because her family had always been a psychotic nightmare. Serial killing would hardly have surprised her.

But Dunne likely had a normal family—whatever that meant, whatever that looked like. So, serial killing and all was a blow. Double serial killing with eyeball removal was a *definite* blow to someone so…noble and upstanding, for all his frowns and attempts at harsh words.

So she attempted to ask her next question gently, when gentle wasn't something she'd ever really had or wanted to be. "Do you have any suspicions?"

He winced. Flat-out. So much for gentle, she supposed. But it worried her that he made her *want* to be.

DUNNE COULDN'T BLAME her for the question. It was a reasonable one. It was just one he'd yet to come up with any answers for. And maybe, if he was being honest with himself, he was running himself a little ragged here. Lack of sleep and too much caffeine dulling his normally sharp senses, so he hadn't been prepared for the question.

Do you have any suspicions? Didn't he wish. "I've

thought about this for a long time. I can't think of one person."

"So like, what was your family like then? When you were a kid."

He didn't want to get into it, but what was the harm? It was all boring, basic stuff. "Military brat. Moved around a lot, so didn't have a real close relationship with the extended family. The grandparents made efforts, but my parents' siblings less so."

"Were you close with murder grandpa?"

She really did have a way with words.

"Sorry, that's insensitive," she said, sounding more thoughtful than apologetic. "The grandpa who did the murdering?"

It was the strangest thing that she made him want to laugh when none of this was funny at all. "I don't know that it was a close relationship, but it was…pleasant. He was kind. He was genial. Not superinvolved, but not absent."

She nodded. "So, he gets arrested and tried and sent to prison?"

Dunne nodded. "Where he died."

"What was your mom's reaction?"

A tragedy. But that was overdramatic. "She didn't believe it. Even when he confessed. Even when he died. She refused to believe it."

Quinn seemed to take some time to think this over. "What's she doing now?"

"She…passed away a couple years later."

Quinn didn't offer any platitudes or sympathy, and why should she? She'd never even known her mother.

"And your dad?" Quinn pressed, focused on the information. On the patterns. Which was what he needed, really. Not to worry someone was going to be concerned about his problems, his emotional state. His brothers wouldn't necessarily *say* anything, but they'd watch him carefully. For all the signs of emotional upheaval he could definitely keep hidden from Quinn, but less likely from them.

Or he was just convincing himself he hadn't made a mistake by letting her tag along. "My father is a higher-up in the military." And one of the few people who knew he was still alive.

"Siblings?"

"I was an only child."

"Are you sure?"

He flicked a confused glance at her. "Am I sure I don't have siblings?"

"Yeah, like, Jessie didn't know about me, right? And we're identical twins. Maybe your mom or dad had some second family. Before they were married, or during."

Dunne thought about his mother. A second family? "I don't think so. My mom was…" He didn't know how to come up with the words. *Subservient* was too harsh. But he had no other words, so he didn't finish. "And my father doesn't connect to my grandfather, far as I can tell."

"Okay, so your grandfather is your mother's family, right? So like…uncles, aunts, cousins? People related to you and your grandfather?"

"My mother wasn't close with her family. We moved

around too much." And she gave everything to his father and the life he'd chosen. She'd been the perfect military wife.

And Dunne couldn't didn't have one memory where she seemed truly happy.

Not that his father was a monster. Just selfish. And maybe that wasn't even fair. Dunne didn't know what had gone on behind closed doors in his parents' marriage. He'd been a child. And Dad had been a wreck when Mom died, so there was *some* love there.

All of it involved emotions he didn't want to delve into around anyone, let alone a virtual stranger who'd forced her way into *his* mission.

"Look, we could go through every branch in my family tree, but I don't see what the point would be. Best to get to Springview and work on information about the murder. Go from there."

Quinn was uncharacteristically quiet.

For a second or two.

"Mysteries and clues aren't just about the facts," she said, as if she was picking her words carefully. A rare attempt for the woman, that was for sure. "Facts are great and important if you're, like, law enforcement, trying to build a case. But we're not building a case. We're trying to get to the bottom of something. Which involves more than evidence. It involves connections, and psychology."

He hated that it made sense. He wanted it to be about facts so he could keep his emotions out of it. So he could just…solve the problem.

But he had been a soldier long enough to know that

even military missions meant to involve no emotion at all, involved people. And therefore feelings and psychologies and traumas he'd never understand even if he tried.

"We can't make sense out of a serial killer," he said, because…well, he didn't want to make sense of one. He didn't want to be able to access that thought process. If he did, didn't that mean there was some kind of murderer inside of him?

"Maybe. Maybe not. I'm sure there are bits and pieces we can make sense of, even if they aren't rational. You should see if anyone you're related to has ties to Nebraska."

"Why would Nebraska matter beyond the letters?"

"Because this was the first. And the date connects to you—you wouldn't admit it, but I'm not stupid. Whoever it was started here, on the day they started, for reasons. Reasons you might be able to uncover if you look into your family."

She wasn't wrong. He was going to have to get used to her pushing him to do things and think in ways he'd been avoiding. His brothers hadn't pushed. If anything, they'd pulled. They hadn't wanted him to go down this road.

But he'd taken the road, so he'd have to accept Quinn's pushes. "Okay."

She sat back in her seat, satisfied smile spreading across her face. It was maybe a little petty, but he wanted to wipe it away.

"How are you explaining this to Jessie?"

She didn't react like he'd hoped. No, she kept smiling as she shrugged. "Probably tell her you were *desperate* for my expertise and just begged me to tag along. How are you going to keep your brothers from following?"

Dunne decided to ignore her question. "She's not going to believe that."

"Why not?" But she grinned at him. Teasing him. "You're definitely the begging type."

He was not a man anyone *teased* easily. Sure, his brothers gave him a hard time, but it was born of years of military service together—including dangerous, undercover operations that had led to them to being erased from public knowledge.

"Yeah, on my knees. Are you going to tell her I cried while you're at it?"

She laughed and he found his own mouth curving, even in these ridiculous circumstances.

"Come on, spill. What's keeping your brothers from following you?"

He said nothing. But of course that didn't deter her.

"I mean, my first guess would be you're all criminals and you've killed together and now have to lie low so no one finds you. They can't come after you or they risk being caught too. But your upset over the serial killer doesn't really mesh with that one."

"Excellent deduction skills."

"Unless it was some kind of justified, noble we took-down-the-bad-guy type deal."

"It was not."

"But you're not brothers, so—"

"We're brothers," he said sharply, unable to stop

himself. If there was nothing else in this life that he'd managed to hold on to, it was that. Them. They were a family, no matter how they'd been made.

She sighed heavily. "Sorry, not *biological* brothers. You came together for a reason. You're hiding out together for a reason."

"We aren't hiding. We're living."

She seemed to consider that. Then pouted at him. He supposed she was trying to look sweet and trustworthy and alluring.

Irritating that she did.

But it didn't last long before she groaned in frustration. She poked a finger into his shoulder. "Why don't you just *tell* me?"

"No, I'm enjoying the guessing. Please keep it up."

She grinned at him again. "No, you're not. You wish I would shut up."

"I do, and I'm wondering how you survived what you did when you never seem to."

"I could have been the quiet, biddable victim. Probably would have saved me a few scars. But I would have been hidden and locked away, or worse. At least loud and obnoxious and brash, I spoke their language, and they used me. Sure, it was a crappy kind of using, but better than nothing."

Scars. He wanted to believe she was talking about the emotional-trauma kind, but he had the sneaking suspicion she meant the physical ones. He hated to think of her, Sarabeth's age, living with that passel of obsessive sociopaths who'd hurt her.

He couldn't fathom how she'd turned out all right

just based on what *he* knew, and of course, that was likely only the tip of the iceberg.

She was still staring at him, but her gaze had sharpened. Any good humor or fake sweetness long gone. "Don't tell me you feel sorry for me."

Of course he did, even if she didn't want him to. "Shouldn't I?"

"Pity's fine enough for people who want to wallow in it." She crossed her arms over her chest and jutted her chin out as she glared out the windshield. "But I don't."

Certain. Tough. Determined.

And yet there was something in her eyes, a vulnerability he had no doubt she'd try to hide if she knew he saw it. It was all the little dichotomies of her personality, ones he recognized in himself, that had him explaining everything he shouldn't.

"My brothers and I were in the military together."

Chapter Seven

Quinn listened as Dunne explained his military past. She didn't interrupt to ask questions or demand more information. No, she bit her tongue, because he was offering her up a lot more than she'd expected him to.

That he'd been part of some special group to take down *terrorists*, but an IT error had given their identities to the enemy.

"They couldn't keep us on the mission, or risk us on any others as long as we were terrorist targets. Neither could they just send us home. This is where having a father in the higher ranks helps, I think. He was instrumental in the plan. New identities. Somewhere no one would think, or care, to look for us."

Though it was rare for her, she kept quiet. Really working through the information, making sure she understood it. And, okay, trying to remind herself that it didn't have to be true. He didn't really have to be *that* good and *that* noble. Anytime a guy told a story, especially about military junk, they were usually exaggerating at best, lying at worst.

Somehow, she could believe neither of him in this

moment and it made her feel decidedly less *sure* about things than she usually did.

When she was quiet for a good full minute or two, he slid a quick, skeptical look at her. "No sarcastic quip? No inappropriate questions?"

It felt like a failure not to come up with one. "You don't think they'll ever call you back?"

He blinked. Once. Not a flinch this time, but still a reaction. She couldn't hazard a guess what it meant, though. Was he surprised by the question because he'd never considered it? Or was it because of something else deeper and more complicated?

Quinn understood with a new kind of clarity watching these men and Jessie and Sarabeth interact that sometimes *more complicated* was personal, and as much as she might want to poke into the psychology of it, Dunne was a real person. With real feelings. Ones she should consider.

So she didn't poke about the military, or his brothers, terrorists, or all the million questions she had about being declared legally dead—such an odd opposite to her having to prove she was ever born. She sat back in her seat and surveyed the flat land as it passed by the window. "So, what's the next step?"

He took a moment, and she didn't dare look at him. She'd end up asking an insensitive question.

"We'll find a motel in Springview, then go get a real meal."

This time she did look at him, studied the hard lines of his profile. He didn't *look* tired, but surely he hadn't slept in something like twenty-four hours. "Don't you think you should sleep at some point?"

"I will. We need a place to rest and some fuel first."

She couldn't argue with him there. So she didn't. She didn't argue or ask questions, no matter how much she wanted to. She rode in silence, all the remaining way to Springview. She texted Jessie that she was safe and sound and keeping an eye on Dunne. She didn't take Jessie's immediate phone call or listen to what was no doubt a scolding message.

It's done. Don't worry, we'll look after each other.

This is unreasonable and irresponsible of both of you, Jessie had responded.

Quinn had replied with a smiley face emoji surrounded by hearts.

Dunne didn't stop at the first two motels they passed, and she didn't ask why because she figured they were too close to the highway. He wanted to remain on the down low, both so a serial killer didn't catch on that he might get followed and also, she thought, because of the whole military thing. He was worried about not following all the rules of his seclusion.

Which didn't seem fair when it wasn't his fault the military had made a mistake, but fair wasn't life. Maybe she'd thought other people got *fair* outside of what she'd grown up in, but meeting Jessie and Sarabeth, she realized fair didn't really exist. You had to deal with the hand you were dealt.

And Dunne's current hand was military erasure and a serial killer leaving clues for him. So, an out-of-the-way motel. Then…

Well, she supposed food and sleep, then they'd worry about *then*.

After another fifteen minutes or so, he pulled into an old-looking motel. A few rusting cars were parked in various spots.

She eyed the place. Grimy and run-down, sure, but tended plants in the planters. Decent curtains in the windows. "I should go in with you."

"No, we should try to keep a low profile."

"A couple is more low profile than you. Especially if it's a woman running the place."

"What's that got to do with anything?"

"I'm far more likely to rent out a room to a couple over a big burly man with a limp and a scowl."

He scowled and proved her point. He looked *intimidating*.

Hot, sure, but you know, not everyone went for intimidating.

"If she's running an out-of-the-way motel, I'm sure she'll—or he'll—take whatever customers he can get."

He was wrong. Quinn had done more traveling around, being inconspicuous than he could imagine. Her whole life had been searching for centuries'-old treasure, going in and out of places like this—often as a foil for the dangerous men she was forced to travel with.

Still, she let Dunne fancy himself in charge. She

might not have known *good* men, but she knew men. And how to handle them.

He disappeared inside and she got out of the car. She watched the world around her with casual disinterest, even whistled a little. There wasn't anyone loitering around as far as she could tell, but it never hurt to act casual.

When she made it to the main building, she stood just out of eyesight, but close enough she could hear Dunne's conversation through the open window.

"Sorry. Might have better luck at one of those places closer to the highway," the, yes, woman behind the counter was saying.

"The highway," he repeated, like he was confused.

Quinn rolled her eyes. Dunne might be Mister Built Military Man, but he clearly didn't know how this part of the world worked. She'd been in enough sketchy motels to know which ones ran toward the up-and-up.

And which ones didn't.

This lady wasn't giving anyone rooms who might interfere with whatever else she had going on, and no doubt she thought Dunne was some kind of cop. Or trouble for the criminals she probably usually housed.

Way too nice a place to take just *any* criminal.

Which meant it was time for Quinn to play foil. She opened the door and stepped into the lobby, if one could call the small room with a counter a *lobby*. It was old, definitely, but clean enough.

This lady obviously ran something besides just a motel. Both she and Dunne looked over at her entry.

Dunne scowled, but Quinn smiled brightly and made sure that no matter how much it hurt, she didn't limp when she walked over.

"Hey, babe," Quinn said, moving next to Dunne and sliding her arm around his waist. "No luck with the Mountain Dew in the machine." She turned her gaze to the woman behind the counter, smiled sweetly. "I don't suppose you'd know where I could find him some Mountain Dew? His favorite."

Dunne had stiffened underneath her arm, but he didn't push her away. And he didn't say anything.

The woman eyed her. Then Dunne. "Maybe at the gas station."

Quinn nodded thoughtfully. "We can stock up once we get settled. Man, I'm exhausted."

"She doesn't have a room," Dunne said flatly.

Quinn pouted. "Ugh. Is there another place around here like yours? Small and…" Quinn looked behind her, then leaned toward the lady behind the counter. She lowered her voice. "We're looking for something a little more…" She slid her hand up Dunne's stomach, and let herself enjoy the outline of each well-defined abdominal muscle. Why not? "…out of the way, if you know what I mean."

The lady's eyebrow rose. "Well."

"He can afford it," Quinn continued, trying to bite back a grin at how stiff Dunne had become as her hand trailed back down his stomach.

"Well." The woman turned to her computer—ancient in the grand scheme of things. She clicked a few buttons, but Quinn didn't get the impression she was actually doing anything. "If you're willing to pay the emergency cleaning fee, I can get a room ready for you."

"Sure," Dunne muttered. He put his hand over hers. She knew he was trying to stop her from moving it around—but he was smart enough to simply hold it there like they were a couple.

Quinn had to swallow down a cackle. She'd never known noble men, so she'd never had any idea how fun it was to mess with them until she'd met the Thompson brothers.

Dunne pulled out a wad of cash, and Quinn had to be impressed he'd thought of everything. Credit cards could be tracked—not just by police or even serial killers, but by his brothers who might want to track him down and bring him back home.

The woman behind the counter's eyes widened, but she quickly took the cash and handed over a key.

He didn't point out that if the room was ready, it clearly didn't need an emergency cleaning fee. He simply thanked the woman for her help and then turned, very carefully taking Quinn's hand off his chest and dropping it as they walked out of the main building.

"Told you you needed me," Quinn offered as they walked to their room.

"She thinks you're a prostitute," Dunne said grimly.

"Oh, give me more credit than that. If I was a prostitute, you wouldn't be paying for the full weekend. This just looks like a tawdry affair." God, she wanted to get into the room and sit down so she could rest her leg.

"Great."

He sounded decidedly *not* pleased. Stupid noble streak, honestly. "I got us a room. What does it matter what it looks like?"

"Doesn't."

"You're sure acting like it matters. All stiff and grumpy." She waggled her fingers at him, and then, because she couldn't help herself, she grinned. They stopped outside the door, so she took the opportunity to trail her finger up his stomach again.

She looked up at him through her eyelashes. "Afraid you won't be able to keep your hands to yourself?"

He showed absolutely no reaction. Simply opened the door and gestured her inside. "I always keep my hands to myself."

She brushed past him, way more than was necessary, and swept into the small, grimy room. "Pity," she said with a fake pout.

But before she could make it fully inside, he surprised her by grabbing her arm. With just enough force to keep her in place.

"Listen, I let you tag along. Quit the fake seductress act."

He nudged her inside, closing the door behind him as he stepped in as well. Well, she'd finally gotten another rise out of him. He looked stormy and angry.

It was the strangest thing, but when he seemed truly angry, she didn't feel satisfied for having poked him into that state. She felt weird, and a little guilty, and she didn't care for either.

So, she did the only thing she knew how: she doubled down.

She kept the inviting smile firmly in place. "Who says it's fake?"

DUNNE DIDN'T KNOW why he was so irritated. He knew what she was doing, and she'd helped them get the room he'd wanted.

But she needed to keep her damn hands to herself.

"Quinn, anyone with a rudimentary understanding of psychology can see it's a way to put men off-balance, so they stay away. Or maybe some are interested enough to forget about whatever they're supposed to be doing. But we're a team—not adversaries—so knock it off."

She blinked, once. Some of the color leached from her face. Like the words were a blow when they weren't.

They *weren't*.

She jutted her chin a little higher and said nothing. She turned, as if surveying the room, but was clearly keeping her face out of his line of sight.

Why had he let her come along?

"I'm going to have to get that Mountain Dew so our story checks out," she said. "Why don't you take a nap while I run over to the gas station?"

"I don't *nap*."

"You didn't sleep all night." She sounded unfazed and detached but kept her back resolutely to him as she moved around the room. "And you're awfully grumpy."

He refused to bite and say he wasn't. "We made it here. We might as well get to work. We'll grab something to eat on our way to the place they found the body."

"Cheery."

But she didn't argue with him and he realized... he'd expected her to. That was why he'd suggested it. Because really the smart thing to do was to settle in. Double-check to make sure his brothers weren't going to follow him. Grab a couple hours of sleep so his senses weren't dulled.

When he didn't move to enact his plan, her mouth curved a little. Satisfied "I told you so" in her eyes.

"If you want to do this the smart way? You nap. I go pick us up some Mountain Dew and a decent lunch. We eat, then we head out."

"You didn't sleep much either," he pointed out, not sure why her sudden focus on the reasonable next step bothered him.

"Did you want to nap together?" She gestured at the single bed. When she finally turned to face him, her expression was nothing like the usual sly grin of trying to get a rise out of him. "Or is that another *fake seductress* comment you're so immune to yet irritated by?"

"Jesus, you're unreasonable."

She rolled her eyes. "I know what *unreasonable* means when men say it."

"Oh yeah, what's that?"

"It means I dare to have my own opinion, or prove you wrong, or a litany of other things that don't fit into whatever box you've decided I should fit into. Well, I didn't fit into any box when I lived with psychopaths. I'm not about to start now."

He wanted to argue with her, and since that's what *she* wanted, he stopped himself. She liked to cause friction. Trouble. He was sure it was some sort of trauma response. Giving into it didn't serve him, and even if she *was* here, this trip was about *him*.

"How do you suggest this go, then?" he asked, trying hard to keep the acid out of his tone.

"Don't tell me what to do. Don't try to psychoanalyze me, when last time I checked, you weren't that therapist Jessie keeps dragging me to."

"Nothing wrong with therapy."

She laughed. Bitterly. "I'm sure that's true when what you went through is normal. *Textbook*. But no one understands what I went through. They can't. The end."

"People don't need to understand to listen." He had no idea why he said that. He didn't understand *any* of the reactions this woman brought out in him, so he supposed that was sign enough. Agree. Get some of that sleep. Reset. "Fine, I'll take a nap. You grab some food." He pulled his keys out of his pocket and handed them to her. "Happy?"

She took the keys and then smiled up at him, some of that fake flirty thing she did back in her expression as she used her free hand to pat his chest. "Ecstatic, babe."

And with that, she sauntered out of the room.

Chapter Eight

Quinn went to the station and gassed up the truck, even though it was over half a tank full. Didn't hurt to be prepared. She grabbed some bottles of soda at the convenience store, then drove around until she found a sandwich shop. The motel room had a mini fridge, so she ordered several in case they didn't want to have to worry about food the next couple meals.

Focusing on each task helped even her out. Dunne had said a few too many things in that hotel room that had rattled her. When no one *ever* rattled her.

He'd called her on the sexual innuendo, when that had always been one of her strongest weapons. And he was right, it was either a power move or a distraction—she was usually happy to get either response.

Sure, it had gotten her in trouble a time or two, but not until she'd known how to protect herself.

Then the whole thing about therapy and listening, like he had a clue.

No one had a clue.

Copycat and grandpa serial killers didn't hold a candle to growing up the way she had. So, he didn't get to tell her what to do or that there was nothing *wrong* with therapy.

Infuriated all over again, she took a drive around town to orient herself. She'd gone through Dunne's binder on this murder, so she went ahead and did a quick ride through the wildlife-management area where the first body had been found. She didn't stop anywhere. She was just giving herself a chance to eye-ball the area.

Eyeball. Probably a bad choice of words.

Once she felt calm and leveled out, she returned to the motel. She took a deep breath before getting out of the truck, sandwich and drink bags in tow, focusing on making sure every step looked natural. If her thigh screamed in agony, she had to suck it up and deal with it.

She used the key and carefully opened the door, trying to maintain quiet in case he was still asleep. She got maybe one or two seconds of a glimpse of him at total rest, but he was alert before she'd even fully entered. She supposed that was the military training.

His hair was sleep rumpled, though, and an odd pang of longing moved through her as he turned to look at the clock.

But that longing wasn't for him specifically. Ha! No way. She was just… Well, she was alone, and watching Jessie *not* be alone was like opening a window into some life she'd never had and certainly never knew she'd want.

But it was all…fake. Not hers. Not… Dunne.

"You were gone for three hours," he said, with enough

accusation in his tone that she could forget about her inner turmoil and focus on being offended.

"Yeah, so?"

"So. That's not a nap, that's a...a—"

"It's a nap, Dunne. One you needed. I knew you'd wake up the second I came back, so I drove around. Got some supplies." She dropped his duffel on the bed, then her own backpack next to it. Then she took the bags of sandwiches and drinks to the mini fridge and set about putting things away.

He swung off the bed. She didn't dare look. He'd taken off his shoes and his cowboy hat, and even though she'd lived in the same house with him since she'd been out of the hospital, it felt...intimate.

She rearranged everything in the fridge, just to have something to do, then reluctantly closed the door and stood. When she turned to face him, he was watching her.

She didn't know what he saw, but she knew it wasn't what she wanted him to see. There was just a hint of softness to his expression.

Because he pitied her. Everything about her.

The anger was back and she knew it wasn't productive. In a normal situation, she didn't really care if her anger was productive. She didn't care if anything was productive. She just...acted to act. To feel. To be in charge of something.

But this new life was different enough, and then she'd added tagging along on someone's murderer-finding trail. It wasn't right to go flinging her feelings into the middle of it.

"You want to eat before we head out? Or eat and drive? I can drive. I know where we're going."

He kept watching her, one of his patented, long silences stretching out.

And there was some kind of power in recognizing she didn't have to break it. She could let him be silent and she could be silent.

She *could* be.

Okay, so she was literally biting her tongue to keep from saying anything snarky, but she was still maintaining her silence.

"Maybe you should stay here," he suggested, with that same closed-off look.

She could argue with him. That's what he expected. But because she was biting her tongue, she had a chance to think through her immediate reaction—and not give him what he expected.

"If that's what you want."

"Now, I… Wait. What?"

She had to work very hard not to smile over the fact she'd confused him entirely. "Look, you made it very clear. This is *your* thing. *You're* in charge. I'm just… what? An assistant? Someone to paw through the boring detritus and find important patterns?" She shrugged and kept her voice very mild, swallowing down any bitterness. "Your call."

His expression hardened, and it was frustration in his gaze. "You want to drive? Fine," he muttered. "I'm tired of driving anyway."

She waited to grin until his back was to her. He disappeared into the bathroom for a bit and she put some food for him into a bag so he could eat while she drove. He thanked her, stiffly, then handed off the keys.

She noted that as they walked to the truck, they both worked very hard not to limp. She understood they were trying to lie low mostly so the killer didn't know they were after him, but the killer was obviously trying to send a message to Dunne, or someone in his family. Did it matter if he knew they were coming?

"We could try the police station first."

"No cops until we know what we're dealing with," Dunne replied, getting into the truck. He made a face about the same time she did—pain from their legs cropping up in unison.

Neither of them mentioned it. Quinn started the truck and headed for the wildlife-management area.

"What are you hoping to find?" she asked.

He took a swig of his drink, put it back in the cup holder, his gaze never leaving the road. "I wish I knew."

DUNNE TRIED TO work through the feelings plaguing him. Feelings didn't do any good. This was a fact-finding mission, and part of him needed to see for himself that the photograph that had been taken of the first victim, supposedly in Wyoming, had really been taken here.

He trusted Landon's computer skills, his matching the background to this location. It wasn't a disbelief thing. It was a trying-to-understand thing. A trying to piece together the puzzle.

Those states—real and fake—spelled out his name.

How had someone accomplished that? Expected him to put it together?

And, quite unfortunately, that was why Quinn was here. She was good at that sort of thing. He was under no illusion she would have actually stayed behind if he'd insisted, but she'd had an uncomfortable point.

He'd let her come because she saw things he didn't, his brothers didn't. He was using her. And it didn't sit right to use her without giving her some...say in the whole thing. She wasn't his assistant. She was his partner.

No matter how much he hated to admit it—and wouldn't, out loud.

She pulled into the wildlife-management area and explained where she'd driven earlier while he'd been asleep.

He wouldn't admit that to her either—that the three hours had done him some good, more than an hour would have.

Dunne pulled his phone out of his pocket, where he'd made notes about the location Landon had found, then directed her where to drive and where to park. "We'll need to hike a bit."

"Good thing you slept and ate then," she replied. And smiled at him, full of fake sweetness.

"Maybe you can be my babysitter all the time," he returned, trying to match the fake officiousness in her tone. But failing, because he wasn't one for fake anything. That's why he tended to keep his mouth shut.

"You need one," she muttered as they both got out of the truck.

He chose to ignore that comment as they surveyed the trailhead. Landon's research had pinned the picture down to an area just off the trail, halfway in.

He hadn't been lying when he'd told Quinn he didn't know what he was looking for. Confirmation, he supposed, but what did that do? Nothing really.

And still, he needed it. Needed the certainty he was on the right track.

Because it wasn't just some deep urge to right an old wrong of his grandfather's. It wasn't even some noble enterprise to stop a copycat murderer.

This killer was connected to him. Dunne Wilks was spelled out in the state letters. So, those people who had died, in some small way, had died because of him.

And he needed to make sure no one else did.

If he could see it, make sense of some piece of it, maybe the pathology of it all would make sense. Maybe Quinn would see something with her brain trained to tease out patterns.

And if it's a dead end?

He didn't know. He only knew he had to keep moving. Keep trying.

"Well, I guess we best get to hiking," Quinn said, eyeing the sky. "Supposed to storm tonight, and we're not adequately prepared."

Dunne looked up too. There were some puffy white clouds far off to the west, but that was it. "How do you know that? Some sort of off-the-grid weather sixth sense?"

She pulled out her phone and pointed to the weather

app on it. "It's called technology, Dunne." With a roll of her eyes she started forward.

Dunne followed. The trail was overgrown, clearly not used very often, but since it was still spring, the overgrowth wasn't too thick. They didn't speak as they hiked, and Dunne noted she was paying attention to their surroundings as much as he was. She stopped on occasion to study a tree or a plant. At times he noticed her look up at the sky like she was concerned about that potential for rain.

But the sky was still blue and mostly cloudless above them. Dunne tried to focus on the terrain, on the path, on the mind of a killer, but walking behind Quinn was...distracting.

She clearly knew how to hike, and quietly at that. She was an averagely put together woman—from her size to her hair. There was nothing particularly stand-out about her when she was still, but the way she moved was strangely mesmerizing.

She had an innate confidence in everything she did. Swagger, maybe. And she used it in all different kinds of ways. To intimidate, to get a laugh, to put herself firmly in charge.

Everything she'd been through had certainly hardened her in some respects, but she wasn't wholly without a softness, a compassion and her own brand of hidden hurts.

Her hips swayed in a rhythm all their own, and as they began to walk up a hill, his eyes were drawn to the way her jeans molded over her hips and her—

He had absolutely no business paying attention

to her in any way, let alone *that* way. So, he stepped around her. "I'll take the lead."

She muttered something under her breath, but he didn't pay any attention to it. Couldn't. He needed to focus on why they were here, not on her. At least not as anything more than a... *Tool* seemed harsh. She was a human being and he wasn't using her simply for her brain.

But maybe it would be better if he convinced himself he was.

He half expected her to try to take the lead again, but when he glanced back at her, she was a few yards back. And he had the uncomfortable sensation she had been studying *him* the same way he'd been studying her.

Not good at all.

So he didn't look back anymore. He followed the path, occasionally pausing to study the map and pictures Landon had unearthed. "I think we break off here."

She came up next to him and also studied the map on the phone screen he held out. She nodded. "You lead, I'll mark the trail."

He nodded. He pulled his compass out of his pack and stepped into the underbrush. The world around them was quiet except for the breeze in the trees and the soft inhales and exhales of their own breathing. Both of them walked quietly. Occasionally a bird chirped or a squirrel scolded.

They'd gone about a mile when Dunne heard the

snick of a tree branch deep in the woods. Likely a deer or even a large, enthusiastic squirrel.

But the hairs on the back of his neck rose, that age-old feeling of being watched. When he glanced over his shoulder at Quinn, he saw the same kind of grim understanding on her face.

Someone was following them.

He felt it, he *knew* it, and yet… Wasn't that too easy? Surely they weren't going to come face-to-face with the serial killer already?

Still, Dunne reached back and pulled the gun and holster out of his pack. He took the time to attach it to his belt. When he turned to tell her to stay behind him, he was momentarily surprised to find her holding a gun of her own.

"Where'd you get that?"

She laughed, actually laughed, at him. "Do I strike you as the kind of woman who goes unarmed into *anything*? I've been packing the whole time."

He supposed if he'd been analyzing her as some kind of threat, he might have noticed that. He hoped he would have.

As it was, he didn't have time to concern himself with that or if she knew how to use it.

"And before you ask, I'm an excellent shot," she added, as if reading his thoughts.

He sighed and hoped she was right and not overly confident. "Keep close. You walk forward, I'll be at your six. We'll stay on our path."

"You don't want to follow the noise?"

"Not yet."

She nodded and moved in front of him. He followed, his back facing hers so they weren't ambushed. It was slow going now that they were anticipating being shot at, but eventually they made it to what Dunne believed to be the clearing where the murder happened.

Or at least where the body was found and photographed. Dunne moved in a slow circle. The feeling of being watched was gone. He hadn't heard another noise that might be construed as human.

There was nothing. No one. Still, he watched. Listened. Strained to make sense of any of this.

"Dunne."

"Shh."

"Dunne."

He turned to face Quinn, ready to force her to be quiet if he had to, but she was pointing at something.

There was an arrow stuck in a tree a few yards away. The hunting kind that could take down a large deer from a considerable range with a crossbow. It could have been left there by anyone—wildlife-management areas were as much for hunting as anything else—but something was stuck to the tree *with* the arrow, and the way Quinn was pointing at it, it wasn't just *random*.

He walked over. It was an envelope. With his name on it.

"You shouldn't touch it," Quinn hissed when he reached out. "The police can get prints or DNA."

Dunne shook his head. He didn't touch the arrow, but he tore the envelope from the point. "I can't call the police if something has my real name on it. I'm supposed to be dead."

He tore open the envelope. Inside was a small sheet of paper with a few simple words typed in a haunted-house-type font:

WELCOME. LET THE GAMES BEGIN.

Chapter Nine

Quinn tried to suppress the shudder that went through her. She'd seen worse. Grown up with creepier things, but that being addressed to Dunne... The word *games*.

Yeah, she didn't like it.

She looked up from the words to Dunne. His expression was flat. Stoic. But he held his body so still, so tense, she knew the move had effected him.

"Dunne," she said, trying to find the right tone that would get through all of that military stoicism. Something firm, but not...authoritative. She wasn't sure she had that kind of balance in her, but she tried. "I know you've got this whole hidden identity thing, but that doesn't mean you can't go to the police and—"

"That's exactly what it means," he replied, shoving the piece of paper in his pocket. He studied the arrow, then took his phone out and took a picture of it, before typing out a message.

"I sent a photo to Landon. And the location. Once the text goes through, he'll contact police with an anonymous tip. It's not the letter, sure, but the arrow might have prints or DNA or something." He shoved his phone back in his pocket.

Quinn studied the arrow sticking out from the tree. She highly doubted whoever set this up was leaving anything to chance. They'd killed eight people at least. All to get Dunne's attention?

"I think we should go back to the motel. Watch for tails. And start looking into family members who might connect to you and your grandfather and Nebraska."

He didn't say anything to that, didn't glance at her. He just stood there with that same tense, blank look on his face.

Quinn swallowed. She didn't quite understand the feelings swirling in her. Something like sympathy and this strange need to help him. When she'd been taught from a very young age you only helped yourself.

But she'd helped Jessie. And Sarabeth. She'd stepped in front of that gun because…well, a lot of reasons, but in that moment, it was because Jessie had been willing to help her. It had been watching Jessie be a mother to her daughter and feeling a longing for *family*. Real family—the kind that cared and protected, not the kind she'd grown up with.

But Dunne wasn't her family. She supposed it was a kind of…guilt or feeling of owing him, and his brothers. Yeah, it was just wanting to repay him and them for how they'd helped her out of a bad situation, and Dunne in particular had probably saved her life with his combat medic skills.

So, she was repaying a favor.

That was *all*.

She reached out and put her hand on his arm, trying to tether him to this place rather than wherever his mind had gone.

He blinked and looked down at her hand on his arm. Like he didn't quite understand how it had gotten there, like he was being pulled out of some kind of daydream.

Or nightmare, she supposed.

She gave his arm a little tug. "Come on. I don't think anything good is going to come from us hanging out here with dark and a storm coming."

He still said nothing, but he moved, following her out of the clearing and back through the trees. Quinn followed the trail she'd left—broken branches, moved rocks. She grabbed the brightly colored rubber bands she'd put on different vegetation.

And all the while Dunne followed, silently. Quinn should be fine, uninterested and unbothered by his reaction. Her stomach shouldn't be tied in knots, her brain whirling with ways to ease his hurt. There was nothing she could fix here, and why should she even want to try?

She needed to focus on the fact someone might be following them. Someone wanted to play *games*. It gave her a cold chill. She knew all too well the type of people who wanted to play games with life and death.

They made it back to the trail without getting the sense anyone was following them. Quinn eyed the sky. She didn't like storms, and the clouds had begun to roll in. There were still bits of blue, but they were getting smaller and smaller. Still, she tried to focus on them to keep old fears and anxieties out of the way.

"When we get back, I want you to take the truck and drive back to Wilde," Dunne said, a harsh order in the quiet around them.

She stopped walking and whirled to face him. "What?"

"There's no reason for you to get tangled in this thing that has nothing to do with you." He walked past her and continued on the trail. "You're not meant to play this *game* or whatever it is."

She scurried after him, no matter how her leg throbbed. "I can *help.*"

"But you shouldn't. You could become a target."

"I've been worse, Dunne," she returned, trying to keep the panic and bitterness out of her voice.

"Listen, this is my deal. It was wrong to bring you. I didn't realize—"

"That it might be dangerous? That you might be a target? Yes, you did. You just didn't think whoever is connecting you to all this would catch on to you so quickly. And I'm already in it. I'm here. I'm hardly driving back to Wilde *alone* and leaving you here without transportation."

"I'll get a rental. I'll—"

"I'm not ditching you. Sorry."

"It's not *ditching.* I'm telling you to go."

"And I'm telling you *no.* I won't do it."

He sighed. Heavily and so long-suffering. "Don't be difficult."

"Babe, you don't even know the meaning of *difficult* when it comes to me."

He turned to face her this time. "Quinn, I appreciate… I get it. You're good at puzzles, and it's been a help, but I thought there'd be more…time before we got to the whole threats-and-creepy-letters part. I'm not wading into danger with you in tow."

"In tow? Please. I can handle myself. It's all I've done my *whole* life. You're not getting rid of me. Period." She tried to walk past him like he'd done to her, but he grabbed her.

He held her still and she didn't like being manhandled. Well, maybe she didn't mind when it was Dunne because she didn't fight him off. She held still and let him keep her in place.

Because she knew…she knew he wouldn't actually hurt her.

"You don't owe me," he said fiercely, his voice low and his eyes serious. "If this is about the shooting—I did my job. I'd do it for anyone. It had nothing to do with *you*."

She knew that. She'd always known that. So why did it hurt?

"I'm not paying you back or whatever." Even though that's exactly how she'd been excusing her behavior and feelings in her head. "I'm helping because I can. Isn't that what you and your brothers are all about? You didn't *have* to help Jessie and Sarabeth. You didn't owe them anything."

"We owed Sarabeth plenty. She saved Landon."

"Only because he was already helping her. Only because you all were trying to *help*. Why can't I do that too? Why shouldn't I be able to help? What's so wrong with me that you think I can't hack it?"

He sighed and let her go, scraping his hand through his hair. "It's not about you."

"No, of course not. Trust me, nothing ever is. So, since it's not, I'm going to make my own choices, and my choice is to stay and help. You can't change that." Since he'd let her go, she strode ahead, following the trail, trying to keep all the weird emotions battering at her in check.

It didn't do to be hurt—why should he hurt her? It didn't do to be angry—she wasn't going anywhere whether he wanted her to or not. None of the feelings she felt made any kind of sense, so she pushed them firmly down.

When she stepped out of the trail and back into the parking lot, she stopped. Dunne came to an abrupt halt beside her. They both stood a few feet from the truck, still and frozen.

The tires had been slashed. The windshield bashed. The rearview mirrors knocked off.

A low rumble of thunder sounded off in the distance, and Quinn wrapped her arms around herself, gun and all, desperate to ward off her overreaction to all Mother Nature could do. "Now what?"

DUNNE COULDN'T REMEMBER being as at a loss as he was right now. He needed to get Quinn out of here—that he knew on a cellular level. All her arguments aside, she didn't belong here. Stuck in the middle of whatever this sickness was. She'd been through enough.

But there was now no clear way to get her out of this, because they were stranded. There were options of course, but then he didn't want to call a rideshare or a park ranger for help.

This would be so much easier if he'd left Quinn behind. What had he been thinking? He'd reacted, over and over again, emotionally. Without thinking things through. He'd acted like a *civilian*.

He needed to set all the *emotions* aside. The connections. The possibilities. He needed to approach this like the soldier he once was.

It shocked him how hard that old self was to access when it had been his entire world, his entire personality for all of his adult life.

"All right. This is what we're going to do."

Before he could explain his plan—walk somewhere else, call someone to pick her up while he dealt with all *this*—she laughed.

Laughed.

"No," she said.

"You haven't even heard my plan."

"Let me guess. It goes something like this—we walk somewhere else in the refuge. The truck is either registered to you or one of your brother's fake identities—probably a brother or you'd deal with it. So you don't want to call the cops or a rideshare service or taxi, assuming we could get anyone to come all the way out here. So walk somewhere. Call someone for me—preferably not law enforcement. Have me go back to the motel and then probably phone Jessie or one of your brothers to come get me while you disappear into all this and handle the psychopath after you."

He really didn't care for how easily she saw through him. She really was too clever for her own good, and underneath his frustration with her lack of compliance, there was a small part of him that was impressed by her.

But he didn't have time for that.

He had to figure out how to deal with her. *Her.* The kind of dealing with that got her to go back to Wilde where she was safe and not mixed up in this mess that belonged to only him.

Him. Alone.

"Do you have a better plan?" he asked. Because sometimes the best offense was picking apart someone else's defense.

"Cops would be my first choice, but I get it. You have to be careful on that score, not just for yourself but for your brothers, and this guy is using your real name and blah, blah, blah. He's out here somewhere." She gestured at the trees behind them. "I think—"

Thunder boomed and she jumped, hugging herself harder as she eyed the sky warily, like it was its own villain she could fight.

"You don't like storms."

Her gaze whipped to his, eyes full of irritation and vinegar. "Who does?"

"I'm certainly not afraid of them."

"Yeah, well, I'm going to go out on a limb and say you haven't been paraded out to a high point to see if you might get struck by lightning," she muttered, then winced, like she regretted that piece of information.

Information he could hardly make sense of. "What?"

She shrugged jerkily, and then in a distracting move, lifted her shirt and hooked her gun into the little holster that connected to her bra. She had a couple very visible scars marring the pale, creamy expanse of her stomach.

When she dropped her shirt, he realized he'd been staring.

She smirked.

"Explain the lightning thing."

She rolled her eyes. "You really want me to tell you all the ways I was tortured?"

No, he didn't suppose he did, but he thought maybe... it would unlock some piece of her that might help him make sense of...something.

"Explain the lightning." At least if he understood, maybe he could protect her from whatever she was scared of, because one thing was for certain, they weren't getting out of here quickly or easily.

"If there was a storm, and not much going on in the way of the search, or someone had a punishment coming, we had to march out to the high ground and wait and see what might happen. Nothing ever did to me, so it hardly matters."

But the fear mattered. And seeing it happen to someone else clearly mattered. Because she'd said *to me* very distinctly. But he also knew what it was to want to hold on to the artifice that a bad thing, a trauma, didn't hurt. Didn't scar. This wasn't the place for her to deal with all the terrible things she'd likely seen. This wasn't the place for her, period.

But she was here.

"We aren't going to camp in the high ground, that's for sure." He pointed to the truck. "Our best bet for now is to wait it out inside the truck before it starts to rain. We'll take in some water from the bashed windshield, but we'll mostly be protected from the elements until the storm passes."

She studied him, suspicion drawing her eyebrows together. "Is that what you'd do if I wasn't here?"

"Of course it is. I'm not going to go traipsing around in a thunderstorm." Which was a lie. If she wasn't afraid, if she wasn't here, he probably would push into the woods. Lightning be damned.

But he supposed the smart, *soldier* thing to do was to hold. Think this through. He was a target now—and someone wanted to play games with him. He needed to make sure he wasn't walking into the game simply because he wanted it over.

"And a truck is a safe place," he continued, wanting to take away the tense, *afraid* way she held herself. "Even if lightning hit the truck, which is unlikely here surrounded by trees, it'd hit the antenna or the roof and just short out the car. It can't hurt us if we're sitting in our seats."

"Are you sure?" she asked, as if trying to sound suspicious, but to him, she just sounded afraid.

"One hundred percent. You can look it up on your phone if you don't believe me."

She sighed. "I don't have service out here. Do you?"

He hadn't been thinking about service, but when he pulled out his phone he saw his text to Landon earlier hadn't gone through. And he had no bars. He inwardly swore. "No. No service."

The first rain began to fall, scattered fat drops. He motioned Quinn toward the truck. "Come on. Let's get inside before we're soaked."

He opened the truck door, though someone had gone through great lengths to dent it so it was warped and caused him to struggle. He pulled the passenger seat forward and pointed Quinn into the back. "Less window damage, so it'll be drier if we sit in the back."

The world flashed and thunder boomed, the rain starting in earnest. She let out a little yelp and practically dived into the back. He followed quickly, only getting a little damp before he ducked under the cover of the truck.

He pulled the door closed behind him, but it took a few tries to get it to latch.

He knew immediately this was not a safe place to lie low. The bashed windows made it difficult to see out without the rain pelting down, but with? Impossible.

He was crammed in an enclosed space with no visibility. Whoever was out there, whoever wanted to play games could do anything. They were sitting ducks.

He opened his mouth to say so to Quinn, but another boom of thunder stopped him. The flash of lightning was almost simultaneous. The storm was really upon them now and Quinn was huddled on the far side of the truck…shaking. And desperately trying to pretend she wasn't. But every time the thunder boomed or rolled, she flinched. Every time the lightning flashed, she squeezed her eyes shut and her breathing became shorter and shorter.

She was going to work into a full-blown panic attack if she didn't breathe. If she didn't settle. And he could hardly blame her. There'd been a time when he'd been young and cocky and certain he knew everything. When he'd thought no one who hadn't been in the military and been to war could understand the horrors he'd seen.

But he'd chosen that. He'd been given the tools to fight, to survive, to attempt to do some good.

Quinn hadn't been given anything, except the learned ability to survive. And somehow she'd done just that. It was amazing. That she could be as strong and sure of herself as she was. That she could still bond with Jessie and Sarabeth so quickly after all she'd been through. That she could be brave enough to want to start a new life.

It was awe-inspiring, really. And to see her shaking because of a thunderstorm didn't fill him with pity. It was more… He just wanted to offer something she clearly hadn't had much of. Support. Kindness.

There wasn't much space here in the back seat of the truck. He was already practically hip to hip with her. Still, he slid closer and put his arm around her and pulled her close.

"You're safe," he murmured.

"Of course I am," she replied, but her voice was squeaky at best, and after another loud, earthshaking clap of thunder, she turned her head into his shoulder and simply pressed her face there.

So they rode out the storm wrapped up in each other.

Chapter Ten

Quinn knew it was no use being embarrassed. So she'd practically crawled into his lap like a *child* over a thunderstorm.

So what?

The storm had petered out. She could breathe again. It was an unfortunate reaction, but she couldn't go back in time and change it.

She apparently couldn't control it. So she had to find a way to accept that she was a big, fat baby in front of Dunne, who was never a baby about anything.

She didn't jerk away from him like she wanted to. That would be too telling. But she eased away from the warmth and strength of him, out from under his arm and then as far away as the cramped back seat would let her go.

And still she felt too much in his orbit, his warmth. Too affected by how nice and safe it *had* felt, wrapped up in him. Even with thunder and lightning and everything that had once been used to torture her.

He'd told her she was safe, and worse, she'd felt it.

But she should know better than to think anyone

could really give her safety. She knew all too well there
was no such thing.

"Well, seems like the storm has rolled out, but now
it's pitch-black out there." The only light they had in
the truck was a flashlight Dunne had turned on at some
point. "What do we do next?"

Dunne studied her with those dark green eyes, a
deep fathomless color that saw too much. So much
she tried to hide behind bravado and irreverent grins.

But she couldn't be a coward. She held his silent
gaze and waited for his answer.

"I suppose we wait for daylight," he said at last.

Quinn shook her head. "You can't *wait* around when
it comes to this kind of thing."

"Sometimes, waiting and assessing is the best course
of action. Like you said, it's dark. We don't have the
kind of supplies we'd need to launch an offensive. Fur-
thermore—"

"You're talking and thinking like a soldier. This
isn't war, Dunne. It's a game. Whoever it is that's doing
this, they want to play *games*. That's not just 'oh hey,
I'm going to murder you and scoop your eyeballs out.'
That's 'I'm going to mess with you, torture you, and
then do the eyeball scooping.'"

"Could you please stop saying *eyeball scooping*?"
He scraped his hands through his hair, a gesture she
was beginning to realize was him at the end of his rope.
Or, as at the end of the rope as a man like Dunne got.

"My point is, we're in the middle of a game. You
need me. I'm an expert at these kinds of games."

"Psychotic, serial-murdering games?"

"Uh, yeah, Dunne. Exactly. My father's end goal might have been treasure, but he was willing to kill anything and anyone in his way to get it. He had no scruples, no morals, and he *loved* to play these types of games if he thought it would get him closer to the treasure."

Dunne was very quiet and studied her in that way she didn't know what to do with. It wasn't pity, which she often got from Jessie or the other Thompson brothers. It was like…he was amazed by what she'd been through. In awe of it somehow.

Clearly that was a figment of her imagination because pity made a hell of a lot more sense. *Pity* she'd know how to deal with, so she just kept piling on.

"I had to pretend to be Jessie and marry a guy I didn't even know. I was eighteen, mind you, and that farce had to continue for *years*. We've got to figure out how to play this guy's game, then twist it to suit our purposes. That's how these types of games work."

"This isn't *your* game."

"Yeah. Always another man's game. Go figure. You're focusing on all the wrong parts. Games are about…uncertainty. I suppose if you need a warfare comparison it's a psychological war—not a physical one. We could follow this guy, track him down. But that's not the game."

"I don't want to play his game. I certainly don't want you involved."

"Then you have to make one of your own."

He made a quiet noise of frustration. "You're not listening to me."

"No, I'm listening. I'm disagreeing. I'm trying to point you in the right direction, and you're trying to get rid of me because of some misplaced sense of… noble duty or whatever it is that drives you. I'm not your responsibility and you don't have to protect me. I've done it all. Seen it all."

"Maybe you've done and seen enough."

"Maybe I have, but here I am. What's the point in leaving you to deal with it when I know I can be of some help? And if I go back to Wilde, what do I have to look forward to? My twelve-year-old niece teaching me how to read? Jessie trying to assure me I have every right to stay on a ranch that has nothing to do with me and I contribute to not at all? Someone else trying to help me get an identity since I don't have one… Hey, that's it."

"What could possibly be *it* in that completely irrational tirade?"

She laughed, her reflexive way of trying to swallow down some of the bitterness, but the laugh stuck in her throat. "What part of that tirade is incorrect?"

His frown deepened. "You contribute to the ranch. And you do have an identity. You just need some paperwork sorted."

"That's just it. There's no record of me anywhere. I'm a ghost. That's the game you need to play. Because if I start messing with this guy—he can't track me down. He can't figure out who I am, because I'm *not* anybody."

"So, you're suggesting I let you go after this *serial killer* who wants to…torture me psychologically or whatever?"

"You are so single-minded," she huffed. "It's not about going *after*. It's about setting a trap. Laying out a puzzle. Get him so confused and preoccupied with who I am and why I'm involved, that he doesn't notice us homing in on who he is."

"I can't—"

She waved off his predictable objections. "I don't want to hear how you can't let me get involved and how it's your thing. Who cares? I don't have any things. I'm always involved in other people's things. At least this time I'm choosing it. I want to help. I want to be part of it because it's a good cause this time."

"You're so sure I'm a good cause?"

She didn't look at him. That would be way too dangerous with as close as they were, as clear as the memory of his arm around her was. She shrugged, trying to shrug away all the swirling *feelings* going on inside her. "Yeah, Captain America. I'm sure. Now, the first step is to get out of this truck."

DUNNE HAD BEEN taking orders since he could remember. His father had been a typical military dad. Clear expectations, little tolerance for deviation, and the total and unshakeable certainty that his orders would be followed.

Dunne had always been a good soldier.

But something about the past year had put chinks in that armor he'd been building for thirty-four years. He didn't want to listen to anyone else. He wanted to handle things on his own, outside the rules and orders and other people's expectations.

He certainly didn't want Quinn Peterson sweeping in and taking over. But there was something about her. The way she did sweep in. Her certainty. Her unshakeable belief she knew how to deal with a serial killer.

He should send her back home. He knew it was the right thing to do.

But how? When she had a plan…and he didn't.

"First things first," she was saying. "We need to send the same kind of message he sent us. The biggest issue is we don't know where he is and he probably knows exactly where we are."

"I'm not going to play the same games as a serial killer."

She groaned—actually *groaned*. Like he was somehow being the ridiculous one. "Okay, Dunne, what *do* you want to do? March in and perform a citizen's arrest? Oh, wait. You can't, because then you'd have to have contact with the police, who might start poking at the fake identity you've got going there. I'd suggest you want to go in and murder him yourself, but that isn't you."

It wasn't, but something about how sure she was— about everything, about him, when he felt not sure at all, rankled. "I've been to war, Quinn. I've killed people."

She seemed less than impressed. "It isn't the same, and I think you know that."

He did, or he tried to. Some days were harder than others. War wasn't black-and-white. Even chasing down terrorist organizations wasn't all good versus evil. There was plenty of gray on either side.

And maybe since she'd brought that old wound up, some of the truth and honesty he never showed anyone slipped out. "My entire life other people have been in charge of me."

"Yeah, join the club. But sometimes you learn a thing or two from other people taking the lead. We get into some kind of medic, war, soldier situation, feel free to take the lead. Mind games and psychopaths? My area of expertise."

"That's sad, Quinn."

"That's life, Dunne."

God, he wished he could access some of her flippancy. He was all gravity and she just let things roll of her shoulders. But he supposed it came from all that she'd been through and he didn't particularly wish that on anyone. And really it was…amazing, the way she handled it. Dealt with it.

But that didn't mean she was *in charge*. "We track him down. Figure out his point of operations."

Quinn nodded. "And I'll happily give you carte blanche on that. I tend to get too impatient for tracking. Then, while we track, I'll come up with some kind of message for our friend. But it would be nice if we knew something about *him*. Or her."

"Women typically aren't serial killers."

Quinn shrugged. "Typically. Doesn't mean they can't be. You can't rule it out until you have proof. We need more information."

"We had service closer to the entrance to the park. We could hike that way until my text to Landon can go through."

Quinn nodded. "And maybe we can find out how our serial killer knew we entered the refuge."

Okay, that was a plan and not all hers. He didn't have the kind of supplies to keep them hiking out here for too long, but as long as the storms were done, they could probably make it a day or two.

They got out of the truck and Dunne grabbed his pack. Quinn grabbed her smaller one and he didn't dare ask what was in it. God only knew what a woman like Quinn packed for a cross-state hunt of a serial killer.

"We'll take the road since it's wet, but if we see anyone, we hide."

She nodded in agreement and they set off with uncharacteristic quiet. Dunne didn't like how out in the open they were, even with how dark it was, but there weren't a lot of better options at the moment. They needed to stay as dry as possible, and tramping through the woods after rain would make them both wet.

When Quinn finally broke the silence, he could tell she'd been thinking over the whole situation.

"All of this reeks to me of family drama," Quinn mused as they began to trek down the wet road.

"I'm sure the victims who had their eyeballs scooped out, thank you for *that* term, boil their demise down to *family drama*."

"Look, when your family's unhinged, the drama includes murder and eye scooping. Or in my case torture by thunderstorm, among other things. The point is it's family related. Whatever is going on relates to your family. So, who in yours hates you?"

"I don't know anyone in my family enough to have them hate me, and I'm supposed to be dead, remember?"

"Your dad knows you're not, right?"

"He's the only one."

"What if he let it slip? Like over Thanksgiving dinner. Oh yeah, BTW, Dunne's not dead."

Dunne shook his head. The way she phrased things amused him far too much. Then he tried to imagine it. "My father wouldn't be having Thanksgiving dinner with anyone on my mother's side, and if he was, he's hardly the kind of man who'd let that slip, let alone say 'BTW.'"

"Maybe you need to contact him."

"Forbidden."

Quinn looked up at him. "What do you mean *forbidden*?"

"Part and parcel with the whole dead-on-paper thing. I can't have contact with my old life, including my father."

"That's sad, Dunne," she said, in the exact same way he'd said it to her.

Dunne thought maybe it should be, but it's not like he'd ever had an *emotionally* close relationship with his father. It had always been more of a…military one. They understood each other, respected each other and were even proud of each other.

But they weren't *buddies*.

He could have retorted the same way she had. *That's life*. But he didn't really know what *life* meant anymore. Everything he'd planned, expected, figured had blown up in his face—over and over again.

And in the reality of all that he couldn't control, expect or even prepare for, he only had the truth. "I guess he'd rather see me alive than try to have a relationship with the pieces my body likely would have been blown into."

Quinn laughed, actually laughed.

"Is that funny?"

"Kind of. If I'd have said something like that to Jessie, she would have freaked. It's nice to be able to talk to someone else who's got a dark sense of humor, or maybe just a healthy understanding of mortality."

Nice. She thought a dark sense of humor was *nice.*

"But I suppose you have that with your brothers."

"I suppose." He slid a glance to her out of the corner of his eye. She walked on, head up, that same expression on her face. Like she could take on the world. He wondered what it must be like—to have no concept of what *normal* might be. He supposed that was why she faced it all with such…well, he couldn't call it *grace*, exactly. Aplomb? Acceptance?

She glanced at him, scrunching up her nose. "I know that look. You don't have to feel sorry for me. I'm just fine. Best I've ever been, in fact."

"I don't think I feel sorry for you."

"Yeah, sure," she scoffed.

"It's hard to pity someone who's got a handle on herself the way you do, but that doesn't mean I don't have a certain kind of sympathy for what you went through."

"Certain kind of sympathy… How is that not pity?"

Dunne shrugged, uncomfortable with this line of conversation and having to sort through all the complicated things he felt when it came to Quinn. But he couldn't work with her on this having her think there was just pity there. "First of all, there's nothing wrong with pity if it's warranted. But it isn't in this case. You did all right with absolutely no help. Whatever it was that got you out, that landed you in decent circumstances, that was all you. So, it isn't pity. It's..." Hell. He might not want her to think he pitied her, but he hardly wanted her knowing the truth either.

But he saw the flash of something—headlights through the woods. The rumble of an oncoming car. "We need to get in the trees. We don't want to risk someone seeing us and connecting us to the truck."

He tried to take her arm to lead her into cover, but she stepped out of his way. "You go."

"What?"

"Trust me. Disappear. Keep your phone on. I'll find you."

Chapter Eleven

Quinn didn't think he'd do it. She gave him a little push, desperate to get him out of view before the driver saw there were two people standing out here. "Please, trust me. I've got an idea."

Dunne didn't stop frowning, but he took a step off the road and into the trees. And then another, but he stopped. "Quinn—"

She waved him off. There was a truck coming around the bend. "Come on, Dunne. Do the right thing," she muttered to herself, willing him to disappear.

The truck came into full view and Quinn put her head down, whistling as she walked. She pretended to just hear the truck and look up. She forced her face to arrange in a hopeful expression and waved her arms back and forth in the beams of the headlights.

She didn't dare look at where Dunne had been hiding—or where she hoped he was hiding.

Please be hiding.

The truck slowed and came to a stop next to her. The passenger window came down and Quinn stepped up to it.

The driver was a man, hat pulled low. Hard to get a good view of him, but the dome light of the truck gave the impression of a man in decent shape, maybe a little on the skinny side. But he was clean-shaven, and his hair was short under his hat. She couldn't quite make out the color.

"You lost?" a gruff voice asked. He kept his gaze down and didn't look beyond the window. She felt reasonably sure he hadn't seen Dunne.

"Not lost, exactly," she said, trying to sound breathless and relieved. "I had a bit of car trouble, and I don't have service." She held up her phone. "I don't suppose you could give me a ride to a ranger station or something? I've already been stranded overnight, and I don't really have the supplies to do another one."

"Didn't anyone ever tell you not to take rides from strangers?"

Quinn grinned, the way she would if this situation was real and not her attempting to find a murderer. "You'd be surprised what no one ever told me."

The man eyed her from under the bill of his hat. It was a long, quiet study and it gave her more sense of his age. Younger than she would have thought, twenties maybe. She figured he was trying to make her uncomfortable since his face was mostly in shadow cast by the brim and he was staring for a long time.

Going to have to try harder, buddy. I am no easy mark.

"You out here alone?" the man asked, reaching across the console and unlocking the passenger door before pushing it open.

Without reservation, Quinn hopped in. He could be anybody. That, she knew. A murderer—the one she was tracking or another one altogether. He could be dangerous, unhinged. And he could just as easily be a decent-enough guy who'd give her a ride.

Either one would get her what she wanted.

Besides, she could protect herself. And if Dunne had half a brain, which she had to admit he seemed to have, he'd have taken down the make, model and plate of the truck from his spot in the trees. He wouldn't be able to follow the truck at pace with the sun starting to appear on the horizon, but he'd be able to follow eventually.

Whether that was follow to help or follow to a stand-off, it didn't really matter. He had her back.

And that was something she'd never had before. Not until Jessie and Sarabeth. Not until these past few months and meeting the Thompson brothers, good men who had each other's backs.

She might not understand it, but she was going to have to trust in it.

"Thanks," she offered with another big smile, purposefully not answering his question about her being alone. "Not sure if it's supposed to storm again, but I'd like to be somewhere warm and dry when another one rolls through."

The driver said nothing. He studied her for another minute and then kept driving. He didn't turn around. He kept driving deeper into the refuge.

A little trickle of fear settled in her chest, but it was the good kind. The kind that kept a person alert and ready to fight off danger. "Do you know if there's a ranger station out here?" she asked.

"No station."

"Ah." She pretended to be at her ease, casually taking in the scenery in the dim light of dawn as he drove. "So, where are you headed?"

"Know a spot where you can get service."

"Great!" She highly, *highly* doubted it, as he was driving farther into the park. If she was a normal woman, walking around the wildlife refuge alone, she sure as hell wouldn't get in this guy's truck. Wouldn't let him drive her farther away from civilization.

Luckily, she was no normal woman.

There'd been no front license plate on the truck, and she hadn't had a chance to look at the back. Dunne would have.

She wasn't sure why he'd pick her up alone if he knew she was connected to Dunne. If he was really the serial killer, she wasn't sure what pattern it would be if he killed another person here, but she supposed he was done spelling Dunne's name, so maybe now it was just about a body count.

She didn't let herself shudder. Like hell she'd be part of this guy's body count. *If* he was *the* guy.

"What's your name?" he asked, driving the same path she and Dunne had just walked.

"Sarah," she said without hesitation.

After all, she had a few fake identities under her sleeve herself.

A few more minutes passed in silence when the lot where she and Dunne had parked in came into view.

Quinn kept her face carefully blank as he slowed, then turned and pulled up near where Dunne's truck sat, slashed and bashed.

The man finally looked at her and she smiled easily at him even as her insides jittered.

Man, Dunne sure was lucky he'd been dealt a partner who'd grown up in a psychopathic cult. Because there was definitely *unhinged* in these eyes, and even if it gave her the creeps, she knew how to deal. She knew how to act.

Besides, now that he'd looked at her head-on, she was almost sure this was the guy they were after.

He had the same exact eyes as Dunne. Color. Shape. Oh, maybe she was looking for things that weren't really there, but she'd spent a little too much time these past few days studying Dunne's eyes.

And if this guy had a passing resemblance to Dunne, it fit her theory that it was a family member trying to tie him to this whole mess.

She didn't try to work out the whys—she knew how few *whys* ever made sense when it came to murder. She just tried to compile the facts.

Fact was, this guy looked a little like Dunne around the eyes—*eyes*—and that was enough for her to assume he was the serial killer.

"That your truck?" he asked.

Quinn smiled even wider and rolled her eyes. "Yeah, someone really did a number on it. Honestly? I'm not surprised."

"You're not?"

"No, I've got this crazy ex. When he's not in jail he

follows me around and does this type of thing. I thought he was still locked up, but guess I was wrong."

"And yet you go to out-of-the way places by yourself, knowing he could be out and about?" There was a scathing note to the man's tone that didn't fit the situation, considering he didn't know her *or* her fictional, abusive boyfriend.

Quinn pretended like she didn't hear his disgust and shrugged, pulling her phone out of her pocket and making a big production out of looking at it. "I'm not letting anyone run my life. Even my crazy ex." She waved her phone at him. "You got service on your phone? I sure don't."

"We'll have to hike a ways to get to the place where the phones pick up service."

Quinn rolled her eyes. "Oh, come on. You can't be serious."

"Why not?" he asked, still studying her with those unnervingly similar Dunne eyes.

"You seem nice and all, but I'm not walking alone into the woods with you, buddy. If you're not heading out of the park, I'll just go." She opened the truck door as she said it. Not in a hurry, not in a rush. Despite her bad leg, she hopped out easily, and closed the door behind her. She didn't act scared or overly concerned. She even gave him a wave.

She felt his eyes on her as she began to walk toward Dunne's truck, but he made no move to stop her. She sauntered over to the vehicle, as if surveying the tires one more time. Then, with an exaggerated shrug, she started to walk back the way she'd come.

The man's eyes never left her. That, she knew without even looking over her shoulder. Once she was a few yards away, the man called after her.

"Wait. Sarah? It looks like my phone *does* have service."

Not likely.

But she turned and smiled and started to plan.

DUNNE CURSED QUINN, and himself, and just about anything he could think of as he silently walked through the wet, muddy woods.

She had an *idea*. An idea to hop in a strange man's truck and travel even farther into the wildlife preserve? What idiocy was that?

She was infuriatingly stepping into every plan, messing it up, splitting his focus. This wasn't a lark, and he hadn't come all the way to Nebraska to play a *game*. He'd come to stop a killer—and she could have just jumped into a truck with one.

And if he thought about cursing her and being angry, he could almost smother the wild beat of panic coursing through him.

Of course the driver wasn't the serial killer. That wasn't how these things went. You didn't stumble upon the person you were searching for, and they certainly didn't pick up your partner as a hitchhiker. It wasn't stealthy or smart.

But the word *games* stuck with him. Because this wasn't a military operation. He wasn't hunting down terrorist cells or even trying to infiltrate them. This wasn't even the unshakeable focus of trying to save someone from battle wounds. He hadn't been able to save everyone, but he'd always known exactly what he had to do to *try*.

He didn't have the first clue how to deal with this. Except move through the trees, trying to follow the path of that truck.

What had *possessed* her? And why hadn't he stopped her?

Well, he had an answer for that at least. It was the certainty. The way she'd said she had a plan, like she could *act* this into all making sense. And for a strange, frozen moment, he'd believed her. Or been rendered immobile by the blinding stupidity of her plan.

Which wasn't fair, he could admit grimly as he squelched through mud and tried to avoid puddles. He didn't think she was ever stupid. Reckless, maybe, but whatever possessed her was *something*.

Quinn had survived her entire life in a group of unbalanced men searching for Wild West treasure. She likely knew what she was doing playing these *games*. She certainly had a better handle on *games* than he did.

Besides, she was just…tough. Smart. Even when it seemed reckless, it always seemed to come out okay for her.

She could handle whatever she threw herself into.

God, he hoped.

He kept moving through the trees paralleling the route where the vehicle had gone, just deep enough in the woods that no one would see him from the road unless they were looking. Luckily there hadn't been any turnoffs yet, so as long as the truck wasn't parked at one of the pull-off spaces, he knew he was on the right track.

He focused on that, the fact there was no way for the truck and Quinn to just disappear because there were no other exits besides this road. As long as he didn't run into a fork in the road, he'd know where they went.

Eventually, now muddy and wet and cold, his leg aching so bad he half wished it had been amputated, Dunne saw the first turnoff. He prayed it was just another parking lot and not an actual road.

He crept closer, careful and slow, trying to ignore the way the cold had seeped into his bones, and the ache in his leg seemed to throb outward to encompass his entire body.

He kept big trees between him and the turnoff, watching every angle for the possibility of being seen. It was a long, slow process, but by the time he got close enough to make out the turnoff, he realized it was a parking lot.

The parking lot where his truck sat, vandalized. He didn't dare get closer, not until he fully assessed the situation.

The driver had parked next to the vandalized vehicle, but not in the spot beside it. No, more of an odd angle, almost as if trying to box the truck in. Which was strange, considering the tires of his truck were shredded and there was no getting that vehicle out of here without new ones.

Dunne crept closer, carefully assessing the tree line and how much cover it offered. But the closer he got, the more dread crept in. When he finally stepped onto the gravel of the parking lot, completely free of any cover, he had to accept the facts.

The parking lot was empty.

No sign of anyone. Except the new truck that had been left behind.

He let out a slow, controlled breath—mostly to remind himself to breathe.

They'd vanished.

It wasn't the worst scenario, he reminded himself. Quinn had that gun on her. In that distracting holster that attached to her bra. He certainly hadn't noticed it before she'd put her gun away. It gave her an advantage.

And Quinn and the driver had to be close. The truck was here, so whoever she had gotten into it with hadn't driven her off to another location.

That was good. He tried to convince himself of it anyway.

He studied the truck. It was nondescript. The plate was too muddy to even make out the state it was from. So after another look around, gun ready in one hand, he stepped forward and used his finger to rub away the dirt.

His entire body went cold as the state name as it came into view.

EYE-OWA.

It was a fake plate. Fake and a little too on the nose. Dunne stepped back and studied the world around him, looking, listening for any kind of clue.

Because it had to be the killer. And now the serial killer he was after had Quinn? How had this all gone so disastrously wrong?

But panic wasn't the answer here. Maybe he didn't know how to play a serial killer's games, but he damn well knew how to track someone who was in trouble. Someone he needed to save.

And then he saw it. One of those brightly colored rubber bands she'd used to mark their off-trail hike before. It wasn't anywhere near the trailhead, and he wasn't sure exactly what direction they would have gone into the trees.

But it was a sign.

She'd leave others.

And he'd follow them all.

Chapter Twelve

Quinn kept up the dumb act. When the man claimed to have service, she went back to him. When he pretended to make a call, she acted as though she believed him. When it "fell through" before he could get to anyone, she pouted in fake disappointment.

Then he promised service if they hiked up the hill through the trees. She voiced skepticism. Took a few steps away from him, eyeing him warily.

She didn't act *too* dumb, not unbelievable dumb. Just dumb enough for someone who killed for fun to believe.

He'd emptied his pockets, promised he wasn't carrying any weapons—though she knew they could be easily hidden underneath the coveralls he wore. The coveralls also hid his body type. Was he a skinny rail under there? Did he have impressive muscles that could overpower her?

But she let him convince her with his fake promises. She made him lead the way and used what she had in her pockets and her pack to mark the trail for Dunne to follow—*that* was the one thing she made sure this man didn't notice.

She knew Dunne would follow no matter what, but the clues made it easier. And made her feel safer.

What she didn't know was if this man thought Dunne would follow, if he knew she had any connection to Dunne. Or was she just a hapless victim to him?

She really hoped so, because, boy, was he going to be surprised if that was the case.

Every few yards, she looked at her phone and sighed heavily when the bars still didn't pop up.

"I was camping just up the hill a ways, and I promise you, I had full service," he offered in the same cheerful way. "Even streamed a show on my phone last night."

"I didn't know they let people backcountry camp in wildlife refuges."

"Well, they'd have to know I was doing it, wouldn't they?" He chuckled and the sound had her stomach churning with unease.

She could handle him. She'd handled plenty.

Didn't mean she *enjoyed* dealing with creeps and murderers.

"What else do you do out here you shouldn't?"

He said nothing, and there was a biological response to all this *wrong*. Her gut wanted her to run. Her gut wanted to put as much distance between her and this man who'd likely killed and would kill again without remorse.

But she knew what she was doing. She wasn't going into this blind. She could handle him. She could handle anything. "Say, what's your name?" she asked, when he didn't respond to the last question.

He stopped hiking forward and turned slowly to face her. His expression was… She didn't have a word for it beyond *unnerving,* without any real concrete understanding of what made it unnerving. "My name's Dunne. Dunne Wilks."

She knew she couldn't react. No matter how many different ways his claiming Dunne's real name affected her. *So* many ways. She couldn't swallow. She couldn't shake. She couldn't even *breathe* differently, but this one… It hit her way harder than she'd been expecting.

But she forced her lips to curve upward and hoped like hell anything off in her expression was chalked up to the fact she'd followed a strange man into the woods.

"Well, nice to meet you, Dunne," she managed, trying desperately hard to sound unaffected. "Though, I'm starting to think the guy who lured me out into the middle of a wildlife refuge might not be telling me the full truth."

"I didn't lure, Sarah. Whatever happens to you, it's all your fault." He took a step toward her and she held her ground even as her heart jittered in her chest. "You have such pretty eyes."

Luckily, it made sense for her to let the nerves shake in her voice—even if he didn't think she knew about eye-ball-stealing serial killers. She took a step back. "Look, buddy, I don't know what you're after, but I'm not interested."

He cocked his head as if he was genuinely confused. "You followed me here, Sarah."

"You said I'd have phone service."

"Oh, come now. You didn't follow me through the woods for a mile just to leave. I don't believe it. I've got food. Shelter. Come on, take a look." He pointed to the top of the hill.

She stayed exactly where she was—both that biological instinct and a tactical choice. Be the damsel in distress. Be afraid.

Let him think he could have the upper hand.

He lifted his hands in the air. "All right, just a symbol of my goodwill. I'm going to walk up there. If you want to follow? I'll feed you, you'll have service or you can borrow my phone, and we can go from there. If you want to leave and risk getting lost in these woods, be my guest."

And then he did just that. Walked away. Gave her the space and time to escape.

It was just as unnerving as anything else. Still, she waited. Not because she wasn't sure what to do. She knew exactly what to do, but she needed to feign hesitancy.

He was playing a game. Possibly *many* games. She knew all about games. And you didn't always have to know the rules, you just had to know you always had to watch your back.

And you could never, ever trust anyone.

You trust Dunne. The real *Dunne.*

It was an uncomfortable thought, and it shouldn't

be. He was a good man who'd only given her reasons to trust him. Any discomfort she had in that area was from her own issue and had no bearing here.

This wasn't about Dunne, not really. Now it was about stopping a murderer.

So she took a hesitant step forward. Looked up at the sky again. She didn't have to feign concern. Were those storm clouds gathering again?

Please, no.

So, she followed the path the man pretending to be Dunne had made. When she reached the top of the hill, she was moderately surprised to see he hadn't been lying. He did indeed have a campsite. And it wasn't anywhere near the area where the arrow and message had been—at least she didn't think so from the mental map she had in her head.

Still, she was certain this guy was the Eye Socket Killer, part two, and connected to Dunne in some familial way. Too many coincidences, similarities and the comment about her eyes…

Yeah, this was their guy.

Now Quinn just needed to figure out what to do about it.

DUNNE HAD TO remind himself, time and time again, to slow down. This was not a rush-in situation. He had to be quick, but he had to be stealthy.

He had to trust Quinn could handle whatever idiocy she'd thrown herself into. Eyes wide open. She knew what she needed to know to protect herself.

He repeated that over and over in his mind. She'd survived a dangerous, insane cult. She'd stepped in front of a bullet for Jessie and survived. She'd put together pieces of this puzzle in days that he hadn't in months.

She was a fighter. A marvel.

Who could barely read. Who was afraid of thunderstorms.

It mixed too many things up inside of him. That trust, that deeply ingrained need to protect. He didn't know how to *deal*, and it was the most uncomfortable mantle he'd ever worn.

But he followed her tracks, her rubber bands, her torn-off branches. When he heard the cadence of voices in the distance, he stopped and oriented himself. Because he needed not just to save her, but to get them out of here when he did.

He'd spent his entire adult life saving. It was what he did, who he was, even in this last year on a ranch in the middle of Wyoming, with a bum leg, he'd done that. So, he had to believe in himself to keep it going.

He still couldn't see them, but he moved in the direction of the voices, careful to keep as much cover as he could.

He kept his own footfalls utterly silent. He allowed himself—far enough away where he couldn't see Quinn or make out the words she was saying—to fall away from *Dunne Thompson* and back into the soldier he'd been. Dunne Wilks. Soldier, sniper, combat medic.

What hadn't he done? And a hike through a wildlife

refuge, tracking enemies not fully known, that was old hat and not worth worrying about.

It took a while. Time ceased to matter in these moments of tracking. It was only the target. Only the endgame.

But then he saw it. The slightly off color—a tent through the trees. Movement, human, around said tent.

He breathed in a slow, near-silent rhythm, moving closer and more carefully.

The campsite had clearly been there for a while. Tent, fire, all manner of supplies.

And then he saw her, and he was back to his current self because everything in him nearly sagged with the relief that she was there. Right there. Quinn standing just a foot or two outside the little circle the campsite made, while a man crouched next to the fire, tending it.

His head was bowed so Dunne couldn't really make out any features. He couldn't discern if he knew this man or if it was a stranger. On some level, he understood that Quinn's theory this person was related to him and his grandfather was the only possible answer, but there was a deep, resonating refusal inside of him.

If it was genetic, what did that make him? If the urge to kill and kill and kill was part of his history, his makeup, was that what made him a good soldier— rather than the story his father had always told him? That brave men stand up where other people can't?

And now was not the time to be having this identity crisis. He had to get Quinn out of this situation.

He surveyed her. She wasn't scared. Uneasy, sure. Careful, definitely. But she wasn't scared.

When he was *terrified*. He wished he could will that soldier back, but it was like having two different personalities and no control over who got to lead the way.

"I still don't have service," Quinn said, loudly enough he wondered if she was hoping her voice would carry.

"You really should check to make sure your provider has coverage before you venture out alone," was the reply. The man was calm.

Dunne tried to place his voice. Did he recognize it? Had he heard it before? Was this man someone he knew? A virtual stranger connected by blood?

"Look, you promised me service. Can I use your phone or what?" She sounded belligerent, while raising the pitch of her voice just enough to betray a sort of shrillness born of worry.

But he knew it was an act, because he'd ridden out that thunderstorm with her. She didn't get high-pitched when she was scared. Her voice got scratchy.

Dunne breathed carefully, willing everything jangling inside of him to steady. To ease. She wasn't scared, so he couldn't be either. She had a plan, so he needed one too.

This wasn't about saving Quinn. It was about bringing this serial killer to justice. And he wasn't working alone. She might not be the brothers he'd trained with, fought with and bled with. But here in this moment, she was his team.

So she needed to know he was here. But how to let her in on this without letting the serial killer in on it?

He surveyed his surroundings. Trees and branches

and all manner of ways to make noise. But a man who knew he was being hunted would check on every single one.

He needed to be more to the side Quinn was standing on. Unfortunately, that would require stepping back and coming around the campsite far enough away he wasn't visible and neither were they.

He started to move, but Quinn spoke and he stopped. "Dunne, listen to me."

But she wasn't talking to him. She was talking to the man at the fire. Something foreboding snuck up his spine. An old whisper he couldn't place.

The fire was crackling away now, and the man lifted his head to respond to Quinn. To Quinn calling him Dunne.

It didn't make sense, but as his head lifted, Dunne could see him clearly. Dunne had the vision of something, an odd memory he couldn't slot into place. Part of him felt…recognition.

And a part of him desperately shied away from that recognition.

Chapter Thirteen

Quinn knew Dunne—the *real* Dunne—was out there. Maybe not close enough to hear what was being said, but she knew by the time that had elapsed and Dunne being, well, Dunne, that he had to be close.

Now that they'd spent all day walking and waiting and playing this game, the sun was beginning to fall. Which meant it was time to stop stalling and act.

The campsite was well equipped, and she had no doubt this guy had weapons in the tent. Knives and guns most likely. Maybe that bow and arrow. But he wasn't threatening her yet and that was the part she was trying to work out.

It's a game. He likes the game. The toying.

So maybe she needed to do a little toying back.

She moved around the campsite, giving him and the fire a wide berth. She lifted a tarp he had and inspected the pile of wood underneath. She poked around at the lineup of cookware he had out.

She could feel his eyes on her, and when she snuck a glance, she saw him frowning.

So she kept going. Right up to his tent. She went so far as to unzip the flap.

"What are you doing?" he demanded. But he didn't jump forward and stop her like she'd half expected him to.

"Just checking out the place," she said, trying to match the cheerful tone he'd used on the hike up. "You've been out here a while."

"Only weaklings and cowards need a roof over their head to survive."

Quinn laughed. "Yeah, I heard that one growing up too. I even get it, you know. It's not always easy to have that roof, but what I learned pretty quickly is that having indoor plumbing is a convenience. I'll take, even if it makes me a weakling or a coward."

That clearly confused him, because he simply stood there staring at her like she'd spoken a foreign language.

"In my experience, it's the ones who want to prove how brave they are by foregoing modern conveniences or 'pushing their body to the limits' or whatever other extremism you want to insert who are desperate to avoid the fact they just need a little therapy."

He didn't have a rebuttal, but he did splutter, and she had to admit that was satisfying.

She pretended to be concerned about his reaction and turned with widened eyes and a hand to her heart. "I didn't mean to offend. I'm *all* for therapy. It really helped my sister after she was terrorized."

His jaw worked, and the way the now setting sunlight settled over his features gave the anger in his expression a razor-sharp edge.

But Quinn always was who she was—which meant she kept pushing. Waiting for the snap, hoping for it. "I bet you've been through some real trauma, huh? That's the only reason people do something like all this. It really does help to talk about it, even if I am a stranger. Bottling it all up can be really unhealthy."

"Don't worry about me," he replied, his voice cold and angry. "I have plenty of entertaining outlets for all my bottled-up feelings."

Quinn shrugged as if she didn't catch the threatening meaning behind his words. She peeked into the gap she'd unzipped, but the dark inside and the small opening didn't give her much. Still, she could rule out him having, like, piles of bodies or eyeballs in there.

She decided to keep moving, maybe see if he had anything behind the tent. Something outside the circle of the campsite. A clue as to what he was up to.

"I wouldn't go that way if I were you," he said, and he sounded so smug. Like he was going to *do* something if she did.

She looked at him over her shoulder and smirked. Let him try.

She very purposefully stepped farther and farther behind the tent. Would she find a body? Would he pounce? She held herself loose, ready to reach for her gun if she needed to defend herself. She kept her breathing even so she could hear any shift of his body. She held herself ready for anything.

Anything...except the ground moving underneath

her feet on her next step. There was a snap, and something swept her feet out from under her. She fell, but not onto the ground. No, Her back landed on something…bouncy, and she found herself swinging upward into the air.

She didn't scream. She was too much a survivor to worry about screaming when she needed balance and purchase in whatever…whatever this was.

She scrambled and wildly felt around before she realized she was trapped in a…net. What the hell? She was caught up in some kind of net, now hanging from a tree. Like a *cartoon character*. She peered down at where the murderer stood on the ground, practically rubbing his hands together with glee.

"Oopsie daisy. You stepped into one of my traps, Sarah. Silly goose." He grinned at her as she struggled to find purchase, some kind of comfortable position. "Man, that worked even better than I thought." He clapped his hands together, like a child on Christmas morning.

"What the hell is wrong with you?" she demanded.

"Oh, lots of things, I imagine." He chuckled to himself. "You really shouldn't be so trusting of strangers, Sarah. You see, you stepped into my game. You came along at the exact right moment. I need a victim. You're the perfect prize for our little game."

She didn't feel terror. She had a gun under her shirt, a knife in her boot, and she'd bet on Dunne over the guy pretending to be Dunne any day. She figured a lack of fear would frustrate this guy, so she only peered down at him and spoke in a dry, bored manner. "Lucky me."

He frowned a little at that. "I don't think you understand the gravity of the situation."

"Oh, I understand. You're going to kill me." *And scoop out my eyeballs.* But he clearly didn't know she was connected with Dunne. He thought her name really was Sarah and she was dumb enough to follow him into the woods. He didn't have a clue all the things she knew—and all the things she could do.

She could use that to her advantage.

And, even better, she understood how much he wanted her to be afraid.

So, she wouldn't be.

DUNNE HELD HIMSELF BACK. He'd watched Quinn poke around the campsite, silently cursing for trying to rile up a *murderer.* Clearly on purpose.

Then she'd walked behind the tent—not too far from where he was—and been swept up in an odd trap.

Dunne had wanted to jump forward, but Quinn had handled the whole thing with aplomb. Even now she had managed a sitting position in the net. She surveyed the man below her with disdain. He'd give her credit, if she *was* afraid, she hid it well.

Now he stayed exactly where he was. Partially because the man had moved closer and any movement might cause a noise and partially because if there was one trap, there were likely to be others. Dunne was usually pretty good at sniffing them out, but he didn't want to take any chances until Quinn had a way to get free.

"So, what's the plan?" Quinn asked, still sounding bored.

"That's a question you should have asked before you got in my car," the man said, his tone oddly scolding. Like a parent to a recalcitrant teen.

Nothing about this man made sense to Dunne. It brought home the realization that tracking a terrorist organization and one lone psychopath required two very different skill sets—and Quinn, of all people, was far better equipped than he.

"So, all this just to kill me?" Quinn asked with the perfect mixture of surprise and disdain. "That's a lot of work for very little reward"

The man raised one hand, palm up, then the other, and mimicked balancing scales. "The best thing about playing games is you never know who'll win. Who'll come out on top. Maybe you'll die. Maybe you won't. We'll see."

"If it's all fun and games, why are you cheating?" Quinn replied.

The man huffed out an offended breath. "I am *not* cheating."

Quinn gave the rope she held on to a little shake. "This net feels a lot like cheating."

"Because you don't understand the game. It's *very* fair when you know the game."

"It's only fair if I know the rules."

"Typical woman. Thinks she's the center of everything. This isn't about *you*, Sarah. You're not a player. You're a token. A *pawn*."

There was a flicker in her expression then, and her hand tightened around one of the ropes that made up the net. She looked like she wanted to kill the man herself. But she sucked in a breath and let it out and relaxed again—that perfect aura of bored and superior back, even up there in his trap.

The man had used the name Sarah—clearly Quinn had given him a fake name. And the man thought it was real. He didn't know she was connected to Dunne in any personal way. That, he could use in his favor, maybe.

Dunne weighed his options. He could shoot the net down easily, overpower the man. Even if the guy had a weapon on him, Dunne could take him out before he made a move. He just needed a slightly different angle to make sure it all went the way it should.

Which was the main problem. He'd need to make sure that angle didn't land him in his own net or something worse. And if Quinn could sit up there, calm and collected if a little pissed off, he could take his time to get her out.

Get her out. This man was *one* man. No doubt armed, but not obviously so. If he had a gun, it was underneath the coveralls. Something like a knife wouldn't be lethal right off the bat.

Dunne had time. He just had to find a way to use it wisely. Carefully. So no one got hurt.

He was far too worried about Quinn getting hurt. It was ruining his focus, making him dismiss options that were more risky.

"If I'm the pawn," Quinn was saying, a surprising amount of vibrating rage coming out when she said the word *pawn*. "Who's the player? Besides you, in all your insane glory."

"You know, that word has been used against me my whole life. *Insane*. Crazy. *Dangerous*. A threat." Now the man was getting angry, and the way he shoved his hand into his pocket made Dunne think there was a weapon in there.

He lifted his own gun, trying to get a good angle on the man without taking a step that might set off another trap. But the campsite was set up well. There was always something just a little in the way of a decent shot.

Except his head. Clear shot. Threat over. Perfectly justified.

Dunne had killed before.

But never like this.

"Hey, Dunne? You ready?"

Gun still trained on the man's head, Dunne blinked over at Quinn. She wasn't looking at the man using his name. She was looking into the dark. Not directly at him, but close enough.

"What are you talking about?" the man demanded, his voice getting a little shrill.

"Counting down," Quinn called.

Dunne didn't have a clue what her plan was, but he kept his gun trained on the killer.

"Three."

He could see she was doing something behind her back. Did she have a knife? Was she cutting her way out?

"Two."

"What the hell are you doing?" the man screeched, reminding Dunne of a child having a tantrum rather than a dangerous murderer dealing with his prey.

"One."

Quinn came tumbling out of the net. She clearly didn't fall exactly as she wanted, but she rolled into the dark of the trees, now that the sun had almost fully set. Dunne rushed forward as she got to her feet. As the man behind them let out some kind of scream and growl.

"Run!"

She was already moving. In the dark of the woods, it was dangerous to run, especially if there were traps, but he noted Quinn was immediately heading back the way they'd come. The same pathway she'd taken up meant there was less likely a chance they'd run into traps.

"Zigzag pattern" he managed to grit out. "I think he's got a gun."

"Like I don't know how to run away from someone shooting at me," she returned.

But the shots never came. Dunne couldn't stop long enough to find out if they were being followed, but the farther away they got, the less any of this made sense.

Dunne kept his gun at the ready, an eye to the surroundings, and focused on their direction. Quinn flipped the light on her phone on, which helped illuminate the upcoming rocky terrain.

"He could see that and shoot at us," Dunne warned. Still, it would be hell trying to run down this particular hill without some light.

"He's not shooting. Shooting isn't part of the game," Quinn replied. "And my leg hurts enough. I don't plan on breaking it."

They picked their way down the hill as quickly as they could without risking further injury. She left the light on when they got to the bottom. He opened his mouth to tell her to kill it, but before he could say anything, she'd taken off again.

He ran after her, but he just couldn't keep up with his leg. It irritated him, but also worried him. Her injury was still new enough she could be complicating her recovery. At least his was old, healed and couldn't get much worse.

He caught up with her eventually, even if he inwardly cursed everything in existence as he tried to silently suffer through the pain. He reached out and took her arm, slowing her pace. "Let's take stock for a minute."

They both stood still, trying to control their heavy breathing. He kept his hand wrapped around her arm. He waited until they were nearly breathing in unison.

"Let's just listen."

She nodded, surprising him for not arguing about stopping or not trying to get out of his grasp.

"Nothing." What on earth was going on with this? "We either lost him or—"

"Or it's all part of the game," Quinn said. She gently tugged her arm from his grasp. "We have to move."

"We should take cover until daylight. With light I can take him out if I need to."

"You could have taken him out back there."

She didn't say it with censure, exactly. There was almost curiosity in her tone.

"The only shot I could have gotten off would be fatal," he said flatly. "We don't know enough for that."

"No, we don't," she said. "Though I wouldn't mind putting a bullet in *his* thigh. Still, there's some part of this game we're missing. He should have reacted differently when I cut my way out. Instead he just kind of threw a fit. Like a child."

"Well, some people are sore losers."

"He hasn't lost yet."

"We can't just stand here waiting for him to snipe us."

"He's not going to shoot us."

"Quinn, you don't know that."

"I do. I think he could. He's got guns, for sure. Somewhere. But he's not going to shoot us. How were his other victims killed?"

Dunne had to give her that. "Strangulation, stabbing or other mutilation."

"Yeah, I'll pass on those. But he's not going to shoot me. I don't think he wants to shoot you either. The game is to lure you in. I was bait. Or I was going to be. Whatever. He's not using a gun. He probably *has* one, but honestly, I'm more concerned about bows and arrows. Long-range. He used it to send us a message."

She had a point there. All of her points were good ones.

"So, if we're not taking cover, what do you suggest?"

"Back to the parking lot. I grabbed his keys when I

was poking around the site. We can take his truck and get the hell out of here."

He opened his mouth, but nothing came out. She'd stolen his *keys*. "How...?"

She grinned in the light of her cell phone. "I'm pretty good at games myself, and not a sore loser, because I *never* admit defeat." Her expression changed, hardened. "I will never, ever be anyone's pawn *ever* again." She said it so vehemently, clearly being called a *pawn* bothered her on some emotional level.

But she shook it off. "Come on. Parking lot. I'll turn off my light and we'll go slow. Just grab my arm or vice versa if we hear anything."

Dunne reached out and took her hand in his. "Not quite. Hold hands. Hear something, stop and squeeze. That way if one of us takes a tumble we can try to hold the other up."

"You tumble, you'll take me down. You're a *tree*."

"I have faith in you, Quinn," he said, and that seemed to shut her up. She stared at him for long, drawn-out seconds, but he listened to the world around them. It didn't appear the man had followed, but Dunne knew appearances could be deceiving.

Eventually she clicked off her phone light, and then they began to walk.

"I trust you too, Dunne," she muttered, like she was ashamed or embarrassed to *trust*.

Which somehow made it all the sweeter. And she was safe. Here, with him. They had a ways to go to reach true safety, but he'd do whatever needed to be done to protect her.

He'd do everything in his power to keep her from being another pawn in some psychopath's game.

If it was the last thing he did.

Chapter Fourteen

Quinn hadn't been truly scared up in the net. Worried, maybe. Mostly though, she'd been prepared. Gun, knife, clever brain, if she did say so herself.

Watching the fake Dunne from her perch up there had given her some perspective. It was clear to her, after having spent years in a group setting, that he wasn't the only player in this little game.

She was trying to find a gentle way to bring that up to Dunne, but she didn't have the breath. Her lungs screamed, her leg ached, and when they reached the parking lot, no doubt both in pain and struggling to breathe, they both stopped abruptly.

In the faint glow of the parking lot's security light it was clear that the truck she had the keys for was…

Gone.

They both stood there in the lot, hand in hand, looking around. Dunne's vandalized truck was still there, but the drivable one was gone. Just gone. Quinn felt as though her brain had come to a complete stop. *How?*

"Did someone steal it?" she asked, because it was the only thing she could think of. She had the keys.

"We don't have time to figure it out." He began pulling her into the trees again. "He's coming after us."

She didn't hear anything, but she trusted Dunne's ears and instincts. And him grabbing her, pulling her away, allowed her brain to kick back into gear.

More players to this game.

She didn't want to speak, because clearly, fake Dunne was following them even if he wasn't keeping pace. But she knew she needed to get it across to Dunne. There were more threats out there in these woods.

A *stranger* could have stolen that car, but didn't it make more sense that it was whoever was working with fake Dunne?

Still, she stayed silent and let Dunne lead her. She had no idea *where*, but she trusted him. He'd trusted her, given her a glimpse into who they were up against. Even when he'd been out there in the woods, he hadn't swept or stormed in and taken over.

He'd let her handle it herself, but he'd still *been there*. He'd taken her hand, and he hadn't let her go.

Which wasn't the point, and certainly not something to get emotional over. She wasn't sure how long they moved quietly through the dark, on complete alert. Dunne had his gun in his free hand, but she'd left hers in the holster for the time being. Her leg had ceased to actively hurt, now it was just kind of a numb, concerning throb. She limped, but she could still walk. That was all that mattered.

Finally, after what had to have been hours, Dunne drew her to a stop. She was cold and everything hurt and she had the strangest desire to just sit down and cry.

But Quinn Peterson had been through much worse than this.

"We'll take a break," Dunne said, clearly scanning the woods for any threats. "A careful one. Just rest our legs until the sun comes up."

"Okay," Quinn agreed. "But...listen, I think there's more people involved in this. I'm not sure he's the murderer."

Dunne shook his head as he scanned the dark, gun trained and ready. He motioned for her to sit on the ground. She did so, then patted the ground next to her. She could tell he hadn't planned on sitting. All his talk about rest was for *her*, but she wasn't about to go with that.

He sighed and sat next to her. "I get what you mean. He wasn't...violent the way you'd expect, but it's him. The license plate on that truck he was driving said 'Iowa,' but thc *I* was spelled e-y-e. It's him."

"Okay, but maybe it's not *only* him." Since he was watching where they'd come from, Quinn studied where they were going. She repositioned herself so her back was leaning against his. "Someone took that truck."

He didn't have anything to say to that, and maybe if they had been somewhere else, a park with more foot traffic, she could have believed her own hope it had been stolen, but the only person she'd run into the entire time they'd been out here was fake Dunne.

They sat for a while, resting, their breathing evening out. The dark deepening, and then beginning its eventual lightening to dawn.

"He's using your name," Quinn said after a while, pulling her own gun free of its holster. It paid to be ready, she supposed. She kept her back to Dunne's so they were facing opposite sides and wouldn't be blindsided.

"I noticed."

"No, not just Dunne. He introduced himself as Dunne Wilks. And…" She trailed off. It sounded stupid in her head, and she had no idea it would sound even more stupid when she said it out loud.

"And what?" he returned.

"There's a resemblance."

She felt and heard him turn his head, like he was trying to look at her. "What?"

"In the eyes." She shuddered at the word, at the memory of fake Dunne complimenting her eyes. "They're not exactly common brown like mine. And it's not just the color. It's the whole…area. Different nose and chin, but like from the eyes up, he looks like you."

Dunne was quiet for long, ticking seconds. She listened to the world around her. Night noises. Rustles, cracks, scurries. But nothing human. Not close anyway.

"I don't recognize him," Dunne said after a long while, his voice gruff.

"Maybe you haven't seen him in a long time. Maybe you never met him, but I'm telling you there are two things I'd bet my life on. One, you're related. Two, he's not working alone. This is a bigger operation."

"Quinn—"

"Think about it. The murders were far apart, in all these different states. You've got the pictures of real locations and reported locations. This isn't just one person's work. Somebody made sure to mix up the locations. Maybe he is the murderer, but the whole plot, the whole connecting it to *you* is more."

He didn't say anything, and if they weren't sitting back to back, she wasn't sure she would have noticed the imperceptible change in him. Not just a kind of tension creeping into his muscles, but something else that felt a little too close to failure. Because all that *tension* creeping into him wasn't fear, it was holding himself still against the pain of feeling like he was guilty by association.

Which crawled under all those defenses she thought were second nature. The only person who ever made her feel all twisted up like this was Jessie, and that was different because there was a weird jealousy and guilt of her own mixed in with it.

This was all...worry. When she'd learned long ago not to worry over anyone except herself. This was sympathy, when she'd learned even a drop of that could get her killed. But Dunne did something to her and she didn't know how to analyze it, stop it.

When she could stop anything.

But she twisted, putting them more shoulder to shoulder than hip to hip. "Dunne."

"I don't have a clue, okay? I don't know what to believe. I don't know what's next. This is a mess from top to bottom, and you shouldn't be mixed up in it."

She itched to touch the line of his jaw, find some way to relieve some of that tension held so deep she wondered if he'd ever be able to unwind it all. "I've been mixed up in worse."

"You say that like it should make me feel better. Oh, you had worse at the hands of your father the psychopath. Wow, I really *am* a great guy."

"Don't be ridiculous."

"Then stop telling me how much worse you've seen and dealt with and been a part of. It doesn't make me feel better."

Quinn didn't understand it at first. Why wouldn't it make him feel better? He was hardly shoving her into situations she didn't understand or didn't know how to deal with. But she realized she had to think of it from his point of view—from Mr. Noble Soldier. Who viewed her as smart and capable but also like… Like she should somehow be protected from anything bad.

It didn't make sense to her, when she'd never been protected a day in her life. But the more time she spent with him, the more she understood the way his brain worked, even if she didn't agree with it.

"You deserve better, Quinn," he said, with a kind of finality that worried her. Like he was going to sneak off and try to handle this on his own when *she* was the expert here.

"I've done my share of bad things," she replied, turning even more so she could see his shadowed profile with their shoulders pressed together.

He turned his head to meet her gaze. "You didn't have a choice."

She wished that were true. In this moment, looking at him, a man who just…always did the right thing, seemed born with doing good and right in his bones, she wished she could be *anything* like him. "I did have choices."

"No, you didn't. You were a child. And when push came to shove, when you had the chance, you got out and saved your sister who you'd been groomed to hate. You're a good person."

No one, *no one* had ever called her that. She'd never expected anyone to. She thought maybe Jessie and Sarabeth believed it, but they didn't understand. Couldn't.

Neither can he. But at least Dunne had been to war, and fought terrorist groups, and done things that made him more adept at understanding all the bad she might have done.

She was weak, and she wanted him to believe she was only a victim of circumstance. A *child*, when she'd spent almost thirty years in that group, doing their bidding. Sure, she'd been tortured and punished and threatened, but she'd had choices. She hadn't always made the right ones.

Instead of explaining that to him though, she…focused on him. Because this whole thing was about him and not just getting out alive, but finding a way to stop a killer.

"You're the good person, Dunne. I don't think you deserve to be wrapped up in this mess either. It's not about *deserve*. Life is a mess. It's about what you do with your mess, I guess."

He stared at her for the longest time, like he was seeing something new when she was the same as she'd always been. More or less.

"That's very sincere," he said, his voice rough enough to have that fluttery thing going on in the pit of her stomach again.

She shrugged jerkily, ready to twist so they were back to back again. "It happens. In life-or-death situations. Once in a while."

"Quinn." He said her name softly, gently almost, and she was powerless to resist *soft*, so she turned her head, but he'd turned his too, and shifted so that her nose kind of brushed his cheek and they were far, far too close.

His mouth in particular, in this faint hint of dawn.

"Sorry," she murmured, but she didn't exactly move away.

And neither did he.

DUNNE HAD A MOMENT—a flash, quick and then gone— but enough of a second to have the thought that if he kissed her, everything would be okay.

But that was dumb, and even if he was going to kiss her—which seemed eight million different kinds of mistake—he wouldn't do it huddled in the woods together, trying to avoid getting their eyeballs scooped.

He didn't jerk away. That would reveal too much of what churned inside of him, and maybe sparkled between them. A dangerous, confusing thing. It was better to gently, carefully ease away.

All likely brought on by the danger they were surrounded by, because of course, they were too different and she was too...

It didn't bear thinking about.

"I understand what you're saying," he managed

without sounding too strangled. "There are definitely some pieces that don't add up, but serial killers don't generally work as a group."

"This one is," she insisted. And there was a war inside him—one that wanted to discount that there was some kind of *army* out there killing people and trying to suck him into it, people likely related to him and the nightmare of his grandfather. And one that knew she was right, because she knew what she was talking about, because she was looking at all the facts without emotion.

Because she'd put herself in the pathway of a serial killer...for him, and he was having a hard time believing that even with the enigma that was Quinn Peterson it was just because she was bored, or good at solving mysteries. She had to be here for some personal reason.

It ain't you, idiot.

"How many do you think?" he asked, because it was better to focus on reality, and this was his sad reality.

"Well, at least two, right? Someone took that truck, and it had to be someone connected with him. No one happened by and stole it, much as I wish that were true. This place is too isolated. But that campsite wasn't set up for multiple people, so however they're working together, it isn't in the same place, exactly. We need more insight into who these people are and how they're connected to you."

There was enough of the encroaching daylight that Dunne felt safe enough to pull out his phone and check his service. But there was none, the text he'd wanted to send Landon still unsent.

"There's no service in this place. We have to figure something else out." In retrospect, after running from the man claiming to be him, Dunne thought he and Quinn could probably have taken him down easily. He hadn't shot at them, and his running attempts had been sporadic at best.

Another point in Quinn's favor that there were more people involved in the actual killing part of all this.

A constant circle of questions that didn't make any sense, and he was so damn tired of it.

"How do you do this? Deal with all these unknowns. It's not the same as the military. I knew my target, and when they fooled us, it was an actual trick, a change in action. It was never…this."

"Puzzles are different. They change on you. You put the wrong piece in the wrong spot and everything falls apart and you have to start over. So you just keep putting one foot in front of the other. Gathering the clues available to you until they make a picture. You uncover more and more of the picture. You were doing it on that board, just… You were trying to make a profile. You need to put together a picture."

He scowled. "Yeah, I hate it."

She smiled, and it was strange to realize she didn't genuinely smile like that very often. Usually she was performing a grin or a flirtatious smirk. But this smile was pure amusement. And it made him want…

Well, things he had no business wanting or even putting into words—even in the privacy of his own head.

"You just need to look at it from a different perspective. Each new piece of information is a step toward an answer. We now know there's a group out there. And we know he's part of the group. So, if we're talking pieces, let's analyze all that. I was bait. Not because of my connection to you, I don't think, but just because I was a warm body. He genuinely believed my name was Sarah, and he never gave any indication we were connected, and I think he would have. He complimented my eyes." She shuddered. "So he was tipping his hand a little."

Dunne had to fight back the swell of anger, guilt, all the tangled emotions. They didn't serve either of them now. She'd made the choice to put herself in harm's way. He could have stopped her, but to what end? She could handle herself. Guilt was pointless.

"He was ready, but not fully ready for me," Quinn continued, like ticking points off. He could tell in her head those pieces locked into place, but this was not the way he solved problems and he struggled to follow along.

"Who could be ready for you?" he muttered, irritated.

This time her grin had its usual edge. "But someone had taken that truck."

"Somewhere between the time I went after you and we got out. There's nothing close to here, very little ability to communicate, so someone close?"

Quinn nodded. "Maybe camping in the refuge too? If it was just one person, it would have to be. But, if it were two? It could be someone in town."

"Someone could have followed us."

"They could have, but then they'd know we were

together. Fake Dunne didn't know that, so unless they can't communicate—which if they're a team they've got walkies or something, even out here—it wasn't a follow."

"So camping is more likely. Can we not call this guy fake Dunne?"

"Would you prefer Eye Socket Killer?"

He sighed. "I would not."

She chuckled. "I think we need to find the other campsite. No matter where they took the truck, there'd be evidence of another campsite, and if they did drive the truck *away*, maybe we could poke around without anyone being in there. Find some clues."

She got to her feet and brushed the mud off her pants as best she could. She held out her hand as if she was offering to help him up. Everything was too jangled inside him to even consider physical contact with this woman—a puzzle in and of herself.

He got to his feet on his own. She didn't even react, just gestured with her outstretched hand. "You're better at the tracking sort of thing. Clear mission. You can lead the way."

He scowled at her. "You don't have to placate me. My ego isn't that fragile."

Her mouth curved, ever so slightly. Almost softly, like she was about to be gentle on him. Which always made him feel far too exposed, and *exposed* didn't bother him the way it should when it came to her.

"It's not in my nature to *placate*."

"No, but you're doing it all the same." He forced

himself to focus on the next steps, on tracking down the next campsite.

Not why she might placate him even though it was *against her nature.*

Chapter Fifteen

Quinn was dragging. Everything inside of her ached—not just her leg, which had almost become completely numb, but *everything*. The sun helped, as it eased some of the cold out of her bones, and Dunne routinely forced some of the water and snacks from his pack on her, so she wasn't starving.

But she just wanted to lie down.

Dunne seemed tireless, without weakness, even as he limped through the trees. Maybe she'd been placating him a little by making a thing out of him leading the way and being in charge of this, but it was clear he was made for it. She'd always preferred the more… subterfuge angles of uncovering a puzzle. Not the endless, boring walking.

Because the bottom line in the here and now was the wildlife refuge was huge, and they were searching for a needle in a haystack.

Which made sense, all in all. A serial killer whose home base was a vast refuge with very few visitors. The people who stumbled across them would likely be alone—a rare hiker, an unsuspecting wildlife conservation agent—easy targets. The kind of targets that might not have that much deal made about them when it was discovered they were missing. Or dead.

"What if all those victims connected to this place?" Quinn mused.

Dunne considered. She was used to working on her own, keeping her theories to herself, so it was a strange, vulnerable feeling to wait for his response.

"Landon got all the police reports though. None of them gave any hints of a connection to each other or this place. The articles clearly didn't connect any of the victims, but the picture locales were wrong, purposefully wrong. What else might be purposefully wrong?"

"Exactly. This could be some kind of warped home base."

"And everything else is just bait to get me to come here?"

"Here or a wild goose chase, *then* here, but you came here first," Quinn said. "Maybe…maybe you weren't supposed to, so they aren't quite ready for you."

"This feels a little 'wild goose' to me." He glanced back at her. "We should take a rest."

"Not on my account."

"On both our accounts."

But she knew he was fine. He could probably hike around for another five days. He could probably carry her on his back while he did it.

"Before you start trying to prove you haven't gone soft, remember you're still not that far out from recovering from a potentially fatal gunshot wound."

She scowled at him. "It's been a month."

"Trust me when I say, that's not long enough for gunshot wounds. It could be up to a year before you feel like yourself again."

She thought about his limp. "How long ago was that?" she asked, pointing at his leg.

"A little over a year," he replied. "The limp will stay, but a month in, I still couldn't walk without help. You're doing great."

"That's not what you said the other day. You said you were running a mile."

His mouth curved, a surprisingly mischievous look that made his eyes crinkle and something low in her stomach flop like a landed fish. "That might have been a creative embellishment to serve as motivation for you."

She narrowed her eyes at him, but God, she wanted to laugh. She never would have suspected him of *lying* to motivate her. And she was warped, because it made her feel all warm and fuzzy. "As you love to remind me, you had it worse."

His smile stayed exactly where it was and *oh boy.* "*Way* worse."

She rolled her eyes at him but couldn't fight the return smile. That old argument felt like some recentering. They hadn't always been in these woods, following serial killers. There was this other life.

Quinn was surprised to find she actually wanted to go back to it. When she'd never had anything she wanted to go back to. It sat uncomfortably on her chest and her smile dimmed, because she didn't know if it was good or bad. It felt dangerous, the kind of soft stupidity she couldn't afford.

"Come on," Dunne said, taking her arm gently. Even though he was leading her, it was more...friendly than bossy. He found a log and brushed it off—which was pointless, considering it was a decaying log. But still he gave her a nudge so she sat.

"Stretch it out. The way I taught you."

She grumbled but did the old stretches. It helped he did them too. They did them together. A team. Maybe a bum-legged team, but a team. Even when she'd been part of something, she knew she hadn't been on the team.

She'd been a pawn. She frowned, reminded of what fake Dunne had said. "He was talking about games, but I wasn't a player. I was a pawn."

"Yeah, you didn't care for that."

She tried not to fidget. "You spend your whole life at the mercy of someone else's whims, you get tired of that word. That feeling." She tried to shrug it away. "But isn't that weird...? Shouldn't the potential murder victim be a player?"

"Isn't that just semantics?"

"Maybe, but sometimes, semantics matter." She mulled that over but didn't come to any conclusions about what it meant.

Dunne nudged her shoulder and pointed up at the sky. "Do you see that?"

She had to squint against the bright blue sky to try to see what he was pointing at. "What? The shiny thing?"

"Yeah, I've noticed a few of those. I figured they could be old balloons, kites, something that floated in here or was brought by birds, but that's the fourth one I've seen. Doesn't that strike you as weird?"

She tried to study it. A flimsy piece of something shiny. She had been looking at the ground—for footprints, around the woods—for campsite possibilities, but she hadn't thought to look at the trees or the sky.

Still, in situations like this you had to pay attention to *weird*, especially from someone like Dunne who had good instincts...even if hers were better. "Some kind of marker, maybe?"

"If they're some kind of marker, someone would have had to climb up those trees, wouldn't they? That's an unreasonable amount of work."

But Quinn thought he was on to something. She stood, still studying the shiny scrap on the tree branch. It waved wildly in the breeze. "Never underestimate what unbalanced people are willing to do to play their games, Dunne." She looked at the glinting silver scrap, then around them. "Something is at that tree, I think." She started walking toward it, but he grabbed her hand.

"Carefully," he scolded. Then didn't drop her hand.

That shouldn't mean anything to her, but it did. They tramped through the woods, hand in hand, toward the tree with the shiny marker on it. As they got closer, Dunne's grip on her hand tightened and he jerked her back.

With her free hand, she reached for her gun, ready to shoot off an attack, but Dunne was pointing again.

"It's a trap. Like the net from before. Look." He pointed at the ground. She didn't see anything. "It's a trip wire between those two trees."

Another trap. Huh. "Maybe the shiny things are

like…signs. To the group. This is where the trap is, tread carefully?"

"I think you're on to something there."

"I could trip it, and then we could see—"

"No," he said, a harsh, firm command. "No more of that. We got out of it once, but it's too risky. We stick together from here on out. Understood?"

She wanted to bristle at the order, at him commanding her to do anything, but the way he looked at her… Like she mattered. Like they were doing it together to keep them both safe, not just out of duty but because he cared about her being safe.

She was reading too far into things, but… Well, maybe she was weak. "So what do we do?"

DUNNE STUDIED THE trip wire. It was rudimentary at best but would be effective if someone was caught unawares. But how many people would be caught unawares out here in the middle of absolutely nowhere?

He pulled out his compass and looked at the map he'd saved to his phone before they'd come out here. They weren't on a trail, but they weren't far from the far boundary along the highway. Maybe a mile or two. It was possible this was a place for a certain kind of foot traffic.

And the kind of victim who wouldn't be missed.

"A simple trip isn't going to *trap* anyone. It's not like the net," Quinn pointed out, crouching to study the wire. "Maybe you'd hurt yourself, but you also might not."

"The way this is set up, you're likely to hurt yourself. Look at those rocks." He pointed to where the boulders were positioned. "You'd have to work pretty hard not to hit part of your body on that, and if you weren't ready for it, you'd hit hard."

Quinn stood up and shuddered. "Geez."

"But you're right about one thing, someone would have to be watching to notice if anyone had tripped and hurt themselves. And a person could likely get away, even injured. It's either a luck-of-the-draw type of thing, or there'd have to be some kind of mechanism to tip off whoever set it up."

Quinn frowned and turned in a slow circle, studying the world around them while Dunne looked at either side of the trip wire. He didn't see anything out of the ordinary on the device itself. But there had to be something. He stood. If he was monitoring something for activity, he'd want a camera. But what kind of civilian tech could withstand— "A trail cam."

Quinn nodded. "Yup."

Without needing to discuss it, they spread out and began to search, carefully avoiding the trip wire. He opened his mouth to instruct her how far out to look, then thought better of it. She knew what she was doing as much as he did.

After a good ten minutes of *nothing,* Quinn stopped.

"Here." She pointed up another tree. The camera was half-hidden from where he was standing, but when he carefully came to stand behind Quinn, he could see it perfectly.

"Do you think they're like…monitoring it, as we stand here?"

They both studied the lens. "Hard to say," Dunne replied. And since it was, he took his gun out and shot it.

Quinn didn't even flinch. She grinned. "Nice shot. Now what? Wait for our friends to find us?"

"No, I think we go disarm a few traps and see what else we can take out."

This time she laughed, and gave his arm a friendly punch. "Now you're talking."

So, they spent an afternoon hiking in the woods, cutting trip wires, disarming nets, uncovering holes meant to sprain an ankle or break a leg. And shooting out every trail cam like target practice.

Still, no one caught up with them as night began to descend again.

"They're regrouping," Quinn decided. "They didn't think you'd come here right away. I think they thought you'd flail around those fake places a bit. So they weren't ready."

It made sense, quite unfortunately. Because he didn't have the first clue *what* they were regrouping. But Quinn kept on with her theories.

"I think you're the endgame, right? So they had this more elaborate thing planned, but now you're here. So final showdown."

Since he'd also come to that uncomfortable conclusion, he didn't react. But his response was dry as dust. "Super."

"Well, sure, that feels gross, but you could also look at it from a positive perspective."

"What's that?"

"You're the endgame, so they're not looking to kill

anyone else in the interim. I think that's why it was so easy to get away from fake Dunne."

She eyed him as if looking for his reaction to the moniker. He hated it, but what else could they call the guy? He handed her the last bottle of water, hoping she wouldn't pick up on the fact that it was the last—both so she wouldn't try to share it with him and so she didn't get concerned.

"What about we call him Brant?" she offered before popping a handful of nuts into her mouth. Just about the last handful.

"Why Brant?"

"A cousin of mine. A real tool. Probably too much of a wimp to scoop out any eyeballs, but I hated him all the same."

"Brant, it is." He looked around the area. "Camp here, I guess. No point in risking the woods since we can't see the trap-warning system in the dark. Maybe they'll catch up to us tonight. Maybe they won't."

Quinn nodded, and much like finding the traps and shooting out the cameras, they worked to set up a little camp of their own, in tandem, without having to discuss much. They both needed to rest their legs, eat what little supplies he had left and maybe take turns sleeping.

Dunne decided to forgo a fire, and Quinn agreed without argument. It wouldn't get too cold tonight, and while he figured whoever was after him would catch up eventually, no point in giving a clear-cut signal.

"You should get some sleep," he said, going for a casual kind of authoritative that wouldn't get her back up.

"What about you?"

He eyed her balefully. "Do we have to have this argument every time?"

She studied him. It would be dark soon and he wouldn't be able to make out the intricacies of her expressions, the cast of her mouth, the way she used her eyes like weapons.

Maybe he did need sleep. He was starting to lose it.

She ignored the question. "The way I see it, we maybe have a few hours, depending on whatever it is they're planning, before someone comes knocking. I don't think they're following us right now, but they might track us soon enough. Likely with the big guns."

"The endgame guns," Dunne said, keeping his voice flat, even as the sense of dread filled him.

"Exactly. But remember, it's a game. So it won't be 'bang, bang, you're dead.' Which is handy."

"Handy, of course." She moved around the mini campsite with such utter authority and certainty. She spoke of murder and games with a kind of blasé comfortableness that told of a lifetime of being involved in just that. He knew she didn't want his—or anyone's—pity, but it seemed wrong that anyone should have lived a life like that, one that had given her the same grim acceptance of the bad in the world as someone who'd seen war.

But she just kept talking. "I'll take a nap. Thirty minutes, tops. Then you do the same. We'll switch off till one of us feels like things are about to go hairy. If you don't keep your end of the deal, I won't be responsible for my actions."

It was a threat—and he believed Quinn when she made a threat. Usually he didn't take kindly to someone threatening him, but he'd also been part of a team once. A team constantly in life-and-death situations. You needed to be able to trust each other, to do the best not just for yourself or the other person you cared about, but for the good of the whole. The team. He held out his hand. "Deal."

She shook it, eyeing him suspiciously. "Thirty, tops. How much battery you got left on your phone?"

"Fifteen percent."

She nodded. "Okay, turn yours off for the time being and take mine. I've got thirty. Set my alarm." She sat down on the cold, hard ground, curled up next to a rock almost like it was a pillow. She closed her eyes, evened her breathing and seemed to fall immediately asleep.

He watched her for far longer than he should have. That she could just curl up on a rock and fall asleep like all of this was normal and comfortable and—

She opened one eye. "What?" she demanded.

"What?"

"I can't sleep when you're *loudly* staring at me."

"What is loud staring?"

"What you're doing."

"Sorry." He shoved his hands in his pockets, but he didn't look away. "You know you don't have to be here, right?"

She groaned, loudly. "My entire life the only thing I've ever *had* to do is survive, Dunne. I don't plan on that changing anytime soon. Now, for the love of God, let me sleep."

But it should change for her. Survival was the bare minimum. Sometimes necessary, but hardly the way anyone should live. Still, what was he going to do in the moment? He had no phone service, no vehicle. She was stuck here and with him.

She'd said he was the endgame. If he took that endgame away from her, she wouldn't be caught in the crossfire or collateral damage. She could clearly take care of herself. She didn't need him protecting her.

He could disappear.

And she would be safe.

Chapter Sixteen

Quinn woke up with a start, her mind jerking into gear in the same moment she felt the excruciating pain radiating throughout her body. Serial killers. Nebraska. Thirty-minute naps.

The world around her was dark and still and there was a moment when the disappointment washed through her so hard and heavy she almost felt like crying. When she never cried.

Then there was a rustle of movement, clearly human. A shadow in the dark, but a familiar one. She had to carefully let out her breath so it didn't sound like a gasp or a sob.

"Kinda thought you were going to ditch me," she offered, trying to manage the relief she felt over the fact he hadn't.

Dunne was silent for a long, stretched-out moment. "Thought about it," he admitted. "But we're a team, Quinn. Teams don't ditch."

He held out his hand to help her to her feet. She didn't want to take it. Not when she was still a little addled with sleep, clearly, if she was thinking about crying.

Then the distant rumble of thunder had her jumping to her feet and gripping his hand. Hard, because her leg nearly buckled under the sudden movement and the pain that jolted through her.

With his free hand, he pressed the phone into her free hand, never letting their joined hands go.

Quinn glanced at the display. He'd even woken her up after the thirty minutes. If her leg wasn't throbbing excruciatingly, she might have actually felt a little emotional over it and the whole team thing.

"Your turn to take a nap, huh?" she managed, eyeing the sky even though it was dark and she couldn't tell if a storm was brewing. "Might want to get one in before the storm comes."

"I'll be okay."

"And so will I," Quinn argued, because she knew he was worried about her falling apart over a little thunderstorm.

Hey, maybe she would, but a resourceful woman could fall apart and still watch out for potential murderers. She'd done it before.

He still didn't let go of her hand or make a move to sit down and take a little nap. After a moment or two, she understood why.

"Someone's coming," she whispered.

His grip on her tightened. "Not making it stealthy, are they?"

"I don't think they need to," Quinn replied, a new kind of panic beating against her chest. She knew it had been a group. Maybe three or four, but the sounds of footsteps indicated way more than that.

"Might have gotten in over our heads," Dunne muttered.

This time it was her turn to grip him harder. "Hey, that's my area of expertise."

Thunder and footsteps seemed to meld and echo in her head, but she had to be strong. With her free hand, she pulled her gun out of its holster and she noted in the dark Dunne did the same.

"They're going to surround us," he said, sounding very military and tactical. "Maybe we can take them all out, if they're really into the playing games and not into just shooting us dead where we stand." He moved her so that they were back to back, but hands still clasped.

She was very glad for that connection when a little flash of lightning lit up the sky. She saw a bobbing flashlight beam off in the distance. No, they weren't making it stealthy.

"If shooting starts, we split up and take cover," he ordered. "Pick off as many as we can, but getting away is just as important. Going in opposite directions, so they're confused."

"That's not confusing. If they're after you in particular they're all going to go after *you*."

He paused, just for a second. "I doubt they'd want you to get away."

"But you're banking on them not caring enough about *me*. Not happening, buddy. Remember the whole thing about being a team?"

He sighed. "Yeah, I remember."

A few more flashlight beams started showing up

around them. Quinn tallied eight. *Eight.* This was so beyond what she'd figured on, but it made sense.

Besides, she'd defeated worse odds before. She tried to remind herself of that as the beams drew closer, the footsteps got louder, and still the group didn't say anything. Didn't shout out any commands. Didn't shoot.

It had been a long time since Quinn had been this scared. The last few years in her father's group, she'd been…beaten down, she supposed. Her dreams of escape had gotten smaller and smaller and she'd just grown to accept that she was probably going to die doing these ridiculous things, so she might as well go out with a bang.

But the past few months had changed…her. Hard to fathom now, but she had been desperate to keep Jessie and her daughter out of her father's plans. She wanted something for someone else and…

Dunne squeezed her hand again and it brought her back to the present. Maybe the past month she'd grown a kind of real-family type situation. She was, maybe, part of a team. Jessie's team. Dunne's team.

Maybe for the first time in her life she'd spent some time actually thinking about the future, about what *she* might want, and it would suck to not start to try to reach for some of it…

But maybe this was what she'd been made for. Dying to help someone else. Maybe it was her penance for the times she'd saved herself. And maybe it was just life.

Either way, she wasn't going to be afraid to die. Not after all she'd been through.

"Quinn. A team, remember? No jumping in front of bullets for me," Dunne said, as if he could read her thoughts. "I'm not your sister, and I've survived bullet wounds before."

"You think this was my first?" She made a scoffing sound. "Maybe we accept that we're both the type to jump in front of a bullet for someone we care about."

There was a weighted silence, and maybe he gave too much thought to the way she'd phrased that. *Care about.* Maybe she gave it too much thought too, but there wasn't time.

"Don't have a bullet coming your way, and I won't feel compelled to jump," she said. "Now, are we shooting our way out of this, or are we playing the game?"

Dunne surveyed the beams of light getting closer and closer, in a circle around them. He could start picking them off, but there was no way, even with Quinn's help, they'd take the entire party out before being taken out themselves. He couldn't see what kind of weapons they had. He couldn't even tell where they all were.

Just the beams of light. Bright beams. Not your average flashlight. Something meant to blind in the moment.

"I guess we play the game."

"My thoughts exactly," Quinn replied, and she sounded almost like she relished the chance. "Remember, whatever happens, be as annoying as possible. It might get you hurt, but it throws them off their game. Be mouthy, fight back, don't ever give them what they want. If they get agitated enough, you'll find your spot to do whatever it is you need to do to get safe. Besides, they're playing a game. They're not going to kill you until they get what they want out of it."

"And what about you?"

"Don't worry about me. I don't say that because I'm going to get shot up and I don't care. I know how to assess a situation, particularly if it involves a little crazy. Trust me to handle whatever this is, and I'll do the same."

He didn't have a chance to respond to that because they were close enough now to create a kind of spotlight on a space in front of him. A woman stepped into it.

"Put the guns down," she said, very calmly. Very primly. It was hard to get a real sense of what she looked like because the lights of the flashlights were bright and harsh in the dark, but he got the impression of an older woman. In her sixties, maybe. Gray hair, sharp nose on a heart-shaped face. She was a little gaunt, and she was dressed in an oddly old-fashioned dress.

He might have thought her a ghost if he believed in such things. He couldn't make out her eye color, but there was something familiar about her. He couldn't access it—whoever she was or reminded him of. An old memory, covered in the fog of years and distance.

She had two men on either side of her, holding the flashlights that created her spotlight, which gave off enough light for Dunne to see they all carried high-powered firearms, except the woman. When he gave his head a slight turn, he counted another four behind him with their guns pointed at Quinn.

He'd like to think he'd been in worse situations in the Middle East, but even with bombs and terrorist groups, he couldn't think of a time he'd been so pinned down and exposed.

But terrorists weren't playing games. They were inflicting terror, pain and suffering. Quinn seemed to think she could outsmart whatever this was, and in the moment, he chose to just…believe her. Unreservedly. Not think about everything that could go wrong.

Just follow her example.

"I will repeat myself one more time," the woman before him said. "Put down your guns."

Dunne decided to listen to Quinn and try his hand at being obnoxious—not his default, or anything he'd ever spent any time trying to do, but he'd spent enough time with her over the past few weeks to pick up on a few things. "Pass."

Quinn snorted next to him.

But the woman in the light simply shrugged and turned to speak to the man on her right. "All right. Shoot her. Not to kill, just a—"

And swiftly, his attempt at being obnoxious ended, possibly forever. What worked for Quinn definitely did not work for him. "We're putting them down," Dunne said. He held up both hands, crouched and slowly lowered his gun to the ground. It didn't leave him defenseless, and he knew it didn't leave Quinn without a few hidden weapons herself.

Didn't mean he *liked* not having a gun when eight people around him all had them, but it wasn't the end.

He wouldn't let it be the end.

"Now, Quinn," he muttered when he realized she hadn't put down her gun yet.

"They haven't asked nicely."

"It's not the time. They *will* shoot you, and I doubt they'll let me mop you up again."

She sighed heavily, but then mimicked his move to put her hands up and crouched down. He could tell, simply by the way she moved behind him she was considering letting a shot go off, just to see what happened.

"I know you're the expert in crazy groups, but I'm the expert in having multiple guns trained on me. If they want to keep us alive, so far, let's stay alive, huh?"

She finally released the gun and straightened, still standing back to back with him. "Nine," she muttered. "Everyone's armed except the lady." When she spoke next, it was louder so everyone could hear. "What is this? Some kind of cult?"

"I don't like you," the woman replied, as if it was a simple opinion. As if they were standing in a PTA meeting, rather than the middle of the woods, in the middle of the night, surrounded by eight men with guns.

Lightning flashed. Dunne felt Quinn tense behind him, but she didn't jump or shudder. He couldn't imagine what that cost her, but she was not one for showing a weakness on a good day.

"Dunne Three and Six. Take her to Campsite B."

"Dunne *Three and Six,*" Quinn said quietly enough only he could hear. "What the hell?"

God, he wished he had a clue, but not only was he baffled, he was downright creeped out. One of the armed men stepped forward and took Quinn's arm. *Dunne Three and Six.*

"They're going to separate us," Dunne said quickly. "Remember the only thing you've ever had to do." *Survive.*

"Dunne—"

"That's it. That's all that matters."

Dunne Three, whatever that meant, gave her a tug. Dunne watched him drag her away, fighting the urge to give Dunne Three a pounding and anyone else who might come along.

But Quinn flashed a grin over her shoulder at him. Like she knew exactly what she was doing. And she did. He knew she did. He trusted her to find a way out of this.

But it killed him that he couldn't be there to protect her against the little hurts along the way.

She had a phone, a knife, God knew what else. Maybe they'd take the phone, and what did it matter with the lack of service, but he trusted her to have weapons on her person they wouldn't find.

The problem was, the two men who took her away

had *guns*. And he was left with six armed men and one woman he just…felt like he should know. But he couldn't think of a single female relative this age who would connect to him and his grandfather in any way.

"I can tell from that idiotic expression on your face you have no idea who I am," the woman said sourly. "It really just goes to show what little loyalty your mother had to the family that you don't recognize me."

"My mother." It hurt, in a thousand different ways, but it still didn't answer who she was. Except family. Related to him, his mother, his murderer of a grandfather.

The remaining six men with guns left had a little circle around him now, but the woman stepped through the circle and came to stand next to him. She even slid her arm through his, hooked her elbow to his and then tugged him forward.

Like they were on a pleasant stroll.

"I held you when you were a little baby," she said, and he thought maybe she was trying to sound sweet or maternal, but there was a discordant note that had a shiver going down his spine. "I've tried to get them all to be you," she said, waving her hand to encompass the six men around them. Her expression changed, soured. "Cora always got *everything*."

Cora. His mother.

"Who *are* you?" he couldn't stop himself from asking.

The woman stopped, looked up at him. Her eye-

brows furrowed and she looked both angry and disap-
pointed in him, which made no earthly sense.

"Honestly, Dunne One. I'm your Aunt Sandy. And
it's time you were brought into the fold."

Chapter Seventeen

Quinn was mostly fine with her chances against these two goons. They didn't have anything to say. Just dragged her through the woods to whatever Campsite B was.

She could have fought them off, and easily enough she figured. Those big guns might pack a big punch, but they weren't exactly easy to wield. A couple quick jabs and kicks, and she could run and hide before they could line up the shot.

First she wanted to be farther away from the six other men with guns, and part of her thought it might be a good idea to figure out where Campsite B was.

Though there was a small, ignored part of her that worried what she might find there. She eyed the sky anxiously as rain began to patter against the leaves of the trees stretched above them. Lightning flashed and thunder rolled, but it still seemed a ways off. She prayed like crazy that the storm itself missed them and they just got a little rain.

Either way, she'd fight tooth and nail to survive— she had a knife, her phone, which she'd surreptitiously moved from her coat pocket to inside her pants—not comfortable, but stealthy. She had excellent fighting skills, and all she needed to do was take out any one of these Dunnes to have a heck of a weapon.

She wasn't going to be Dunne's reason to be a martyr. If she was in over her head, it was hardly the first time.

She saw lights in the distance. Clearly it was the campsite they were taking her to. "So, how many of these camps are there?" she asked into the dark. The rain was coming harder now, making her shiver.

Neither Dunne answered. They just kept leading her toward the light.

"You guys *can* talk, right? This isn't some tongues-cut-out situation?"

Still, they said nothing. In the beams of their flashlishts she made out blank expressions and dead eyes.

And various resemblances to Dunne. Of course, she was looking for the resemblance. Maybe she was fooling herself.

But the whole both-of-them-named-Dunne thing—with a number, like maybe all the men were named Dunne, yeah, it all spoke to a blood connection she knew was really going to bother the real Dunne.

As they reached the flickering light of campfire, Quinn's stomach began to twist in worried knots. Campsite B appeared to be the original fake Dunne's campsite she'd already been to. A boom of thunder had her flinching against her will.

Fake Dunne stepped out of his tent, and she went

downright cold. He clapped when he saw her and did a little celebratory jig. "You're my prize. I won the game."

She knew she couldn't let her discomfort show, but it was harder than usual to find her customary flippancy. Once she was sure she could, she smirked at him. "How'd you do that, buddy?"

"I played the game. I'm very good at the game." He pointed to a large tree. "Tie her up there."

She was roughly grabbed, one Dunne per arm, and dragged over to the tree. She fought back this time. She shouldn't, but it was a kind of blind panic. She didn't want to be tied up. Not with lightning flashing in the distance. Not separated from Dunne.

But they were stronger than her, especially when she was fighting from a place of panic, not strategy. She had to *think*. She had to be stronger than the storm and old trauma. She had to be *smart*.

They struggled to tie her up, and in that struggle, she was able to keep her wrists farther apart, keep her muscles tensed so she could create some gaps to work through. All the while, she acted like she was being significantly more outmuscled than she was. She really poured on the drama.

The Dunne army didn't strike her as *smart*. But maybe that was just because they refused to speak. She didn't really know what to think, so she simply worked to keep herself at the best advantage she could while tied up.

Once they were satisfied, they stepped away, though they kept their guns trained on her. Fake Dunne moved forward. Until they were practically nose to nose. This close, she could catalogue the similarities to real Dunne up close. The same dark green eyes, a shade she could only ever remember seeing on Dunne. The way they were hooded under strong eyebrows.

His chin was different, his nose similar but clearly never broken like Dunne's had been.

"Do you want to see my collection?" Fake Dunne asked, so close she could feel his breath on her face.

She had to swallow to speak without stuttering. "No. No, I don't."

He pouted, like a small child, and she actually felt… bad for him. He wasn't right. He needed some serious help. Instead he was being used as some weird pawn in his family's insanity.

He'd introduced himself as *Dunne*, but the creepy lady from before had referred to her little soldiers by number. "What's your number?"

He scowled, first at her, and then at the two men with guns pointed at her. "I don't have a number. I'm *better*."

The rain started to fall harder, so hard it put out the campfire and thrust them into darkness for a second.

Quinn squeezed her eyes shut. She didn't want to see the lightning flash against the dark. Didn't want to be here. She started to pull at her bonds, but again from the panic beating through her, not with any sense or reason.

She sucked in a breath. *Okay, okay. You're okay.* She thought of when Dunne had held her back in the truck. He'd told her it would be okay and she knew it would be. It had to be. Maybe she was tied to a tree, and lightning could hit the tree, but it wasn't like growing up. It wasn't an open field. There were lots of places that lightning could hit.

She was going to be fine. She had to be fine. For Dunne.

She opened her eyes. Rain pelted her, cold and uncomfortable. Fake Dunne now held an umbrella while the gun twins were taking turns putting on ponchos.

"You guys sure are prepared," she managed, though her voice sounded rustier than she would prefer.

"The rain will help," Fake Dunne said. "You'll be cold. Hungry. Thirsty." He was close again, staring at her with Dunne's eyes. "It'll only take a day or two for you to be docile enough."

Quinn laughed. "Docile? Buddy, you don't know me at all."

He reached out and touched her face. She'd been touched in a million ways she didn't want to be touched in her life, but this was by far the most terrifying. Because she didn't have a clue what he wanted from her.

He traced the shape of her eye. Quinn shuddered, no matter how hard she tried not to. But the storm, the whole *eye* thing. She wanted to scream, and she knew it wouldn't matter. Screaming wouldn't change anything.

The only change she could make was escaping, and she had to choose her moment.

His smile didn't falter. "There are ways to wear you down and out. There are ways to make you ready soon. But you still have to be breathing for it to feel right."

Quinn tried to sound strong when she spoke, but she failed miserably. "For what to feel right?"

"I need your eyes. Pretty brown eyes. It'll round out my collection quite nicely."

DUNNE KNEW HE didn't have a chance against six men with guns. At least, not right away. He could maybe develop a plan, but right now his brain couldn't seem to function beyond *your Aunt Sandy*.

It was a vague memory. That his mother had a sister. That maybe when he'd been very, very young she'd been a part of their lives, but then she hadn't. So much so, Dunne had forgotten she even existed.

"I don't understand any of this."

Sandy laughed, and there was a painful shard of memory because it sounded so much like his mother's laugh. His childhood. He'd had a certain amount of resentment over the way she'd made herself small for his exacting father, but she had been the softness in his youth. The kindness.

Thinking about his mother was a distraction from the current situation. Being led through the woods with six heavy-duty guns pointed at him, all at his apparently unbalanced aunt's behest.

He studied her. There was a resemblance, but not much of one. Maybe it was age, or maybe time had erased a solid memory of his mother.

"If you're my aunt," he said, trying to borrow some of Quinn's irreverence, "why don't I remember you?"

"You remember me," she replied, waving one hand

in the air as the rain began to pick up. She reacted to the weather not at all. "You just don't remember."

He opened his mouth to point out that didn't make sense, but he realized she'd probably just laugh again. Things making sense wasn't the name of the game— unfortunately that wasn't his expertise.

Which reminded him of Quinn's, and her advice about being obnoxious. It hadn't served him well yet, but maybe he'd keep trying until something gave.

"I don't remember you, and it seems like if you were really my mother's sister, you would have been at her funeral. You'd have sent the occasional card. I'd have memories of you at holidays." *Maybe you'd know I'm supposed to be dead.* "But I don't."

"I held you when you were a baby," she repeated. "I tried to do the test when you were three or four, but Cora interrupted." She rolled her eyes in almost the same way he'd seen Zara do when she was frustrated with Hazeleigh. Sisterly contempt. "She thought the test was over-the-top, but she didn't understand, because she was *so* perfect." The affectionate frustration turned bitter, and quickly. "I could never break her."

The test. What kind of horror had he been born into? "I'm pretty good at tests," he offered, but he couldn't match Quinn's irreverence, her grins, the way she dealt with people. He wished she was here, right here, for quite a few reasons. To know she was safe, to have a team to depend on, but mostly so she could say something outrageous that would piss everyone off.

Sandy beamed up at him. "I bet you are. You're Cora's perfect little boy. And she did it in *one* shot." She waved to the men around her. "It took me nine tries, and none of them were right. Before you. After you. None of them were good enough. So, that was when I realized… I needed you. I have to break you. To prove you're not perfect. Cora wasn't *perfect*. It's in all of us."

The men holding guns didn't seem to be offended by this. Dunne wasn't even sure they were listening. They moved and behaved like *robots*.

But she'd said nine tries, when there'd only been eight of these man-robots with guns. Dunne realized that in all the people they'd seen, the man with the Eye-owa license plate wasn't one of them.

He was number nine.

"So, where is Dunne Nine?" he offered, though it disturbed him beyond measure they all had the same name as him, numbered or not.

"He isn't numbered. The ninth try was special. Not perfect, but so like your grandfather. None of the killer spirit, but still warped in all the best ways. You'll meet him soon enough. When you pass the test, when I break you, we'll all be a big, happy family. With all the right pieces. And it'll be worth all the pain and suffering."

Sandy gestured and the men in front of them parted. It was a clearing set up a lot like the campsite Quinn had originally been taken to, but with various differences.

There were two tents. It looked like a fire had been going, but the rain had taken care of that. Dunne tried not to think of Quinn struggling with the storm, but it was a physical ache that he couldn't be there to hold her hand through it.

"Tie him up."

Four men moved forward while two men kept their guns trained on him. Dunne considered fighting them off. He wasn't sure Sandy would really be okay with shooting him dead here, when she had tests and who knew what other kind of insanity waiting for him. Which meant he'd have a chance to escape. Find Quinn. Get out of here.

But that didn't solve anything. It didn't end whatever this was and they needed to end it. The murder, the death, the torture. It had to end.

So, he let himself be tied to the tree, though he did what he could to keep the bonds from being too tight or impossible to get out of—spread his legs, tensed his muscles, all the old tricks.

This wasn't all that different. He had the skills to survive this, and Quinn had the skills to survive a couple guys too. Lightning flashed and thunder boomed as if reminding him that she wasn't as tough as she liked to pretend.

But she'd been surviving her whole life, and if she survived this… Well, he'd just have to do whatever it took to make sure survival was the bare minimum for her from here on out.

"If we're family, why are you tying me to a tree?"

Sandy tutted. "You're supposed to be so military smart. I know you don't trust me, or your cousins. You're not ready to join the family yet. You have to pass the test first. You have to break."

She made a motion and the men began to move around the campsite. One held a large umbrella over her while the rain soaked through Dunne's clothes, definitely colder than he'd like. One disappeared into a tent. One put up a mobile awning–type thing and then attempted to relight the fire, while another one arranged battery-powered lanterns around the tree so Dunne was as illuminated as Sandy.

Dunne looked at her and still didn't know what to think. "Did my mother take the test?"

Her placid expression tightened, and when she clasped her hands together in front of her, it was with a ferocity that made her knuckles white. "Cora was always so perfect. She didn't squeeze the life out of things. She didn't leave blood trails throughout the house. She got to be perfect, and I had to inherit the murder gene."

Murder gene? "I don't think that's a thing."

"It's a thing! It's damn well a thing!" She stomped her foot, mud splattering up against her skirt. "Our father killed people, did gruesome things! I would have been normal, but I can't help it! Cora was so sure she could resist the need. Mother saved her, but not me. I gave my sons everything, but they all chose violence. I even tried giving you a brother instead of a cousin."

Dunne's body went cold. A brother would mean... "What?" he croaked.

"It's amazing what a man will do when mired in grief." She smirked at him. "Not that your father knew what he was doing at the time. But that Dunne was a failure like the rest, no matter that your father was the father."

She was lying to mess with him. She had to be.

Then, when he was the most off-kilter and distracted, trying to work through his *father* sleeping with this… this woman, she approached, one of the Dunnes following her with the umbrella.

She reached out and rested her cold hand against his cheek.

"It's time for the test, Dunne." Sandy smiled at him, and if *anything* was different about the situation, she might appear the doting aunt.

"And if I don't pass?" he managed to ask, trying to put everything about his father, and mother, for that matter, out of his mind.

She smiled, as if infused with pure joy. "That's the best part, you're already halfway to passing. You just need to take it a few more steps. You'll get there. If not?" She shrugged, but when she spoke, she was very grave. "Everything is lost."

Chapter Eighteen

Quinn was starting to get *really* nervous. Part of it was the relentless lightning and thunder and how she was completely waterlogged and shivering. She was definitely not at her best for quite a few reasons—add in the whole excruciating pain in her leg and, well, she had *some* concerns.

But the main one in the moment was the lineup of tools fake Dunne was organizing on a table. Like a surgeon getting ready for a procedure.

She had a really bad feeling she was going to be the procedure if she didn't get out of here.

"So, what is all this stuff, bud?"

"My name is *Dunne*," he said distinctly, caressing one particularly sharp-looking implement like it was a lover.

Quinn eyed the two Dunnes with guns and started the work of trying to get at least one hand free from the bond to the tree. "Where's *my* Dunne?" *My* Dunne. That was a laugh.

He turned to face her, holding one of the scalpel-looking things in one hand. Thunder rolled and for a moment all Quinn could think was this was how she was going to go out. A storm around her, tied to a tree while some lunatic cut out her eyes.

She'd always assumed she'd die young, and she wouldn't have been surprised in any myriad of strange ways. She just figured it'd either be in the pursuit of her father's obsession with old, historic gold or because she tried to escape.

She'd never dreamed she'd actually get out of her family's insanity only to be thrust into someone else's. No, *thrust* wasn't the right word. She'd jumped in feet first. Needing something to do. Needing to feel like she mattered.

And now she was going to die gruesomely.

And Dunne? Lord, would that man spend the rest of his life mired in martyred nonsense. She could practically hear him in that stoic, blank voice. *It's all my fault. I will wear a hair shirt for the remainder of my life.*

Because he'd live. She just had no doubt he would.

"I wouldn't worry about him," fake Dunne said eventually, his eyebrows drawing together as he frowned. "He shouldn't matter so much."

Quinn grabbed on to that, because she sensed the glimmer of some kind of…discontent there. A rift in this very strange conglomeration of *Dunnes*. "Why are you *all* named Dunne? Isn't that confusing?" And insane.

"I'm the only true Dunne."

Quinn snuck a glance at the two men with guns. They didn't react to that statement at all.

"What makes a true Dunne?"

He took a step toward her and she desperately worked to get a hand free, all without moving too much, so he wouldn't figure out what she was doing. But she was a little bit in shadow.

At least until the lightning flashed. She flinched. The colder she was, the more afraid she was of the scalpel implement in his hand, the more she had a hard time fighting off her reaction to the storm.

Fake Dunne stepped forward, studying her face.

"Are you afraid of the storm?" he asked, and there was almost a note of sympathy. Or at least, curiosity. Nothing mean. But he was getting closer with that knife thing, and that was suddenly worse than the potential for getting hit by lightning.

She looked at him. He wasn't *well*, that was clear. But he hadn't shot at her when he'd had the chance. Hadn't hit her or been violent in any way. He wasn't like her normal adversary.

"Yes," she managed to say, though it was hard to admit it. "Had a few bad experiences with lightning."

He nodded, like he understood. "Bad experiences shape us." He kept stepping closer and closer. The metal in his hand glinting in the beams of the flashlight and the intermittent lightning.

"I've had my fair share. How about you?"

Something in his expression shuttered, and he slid a look to the two men with guns. "I'm special," he said. "Grandpa thought so. Mother thinks so. When you're special, you have a great responsibility to the family name."

"My family name is a bunch of murdering morons who chased after a boogeyman my entire life, and when they figured out it was real, it ruined them."

"Murdering." He pursed his lips together. "I don't approve of murder. That's what makes me special."

She laughed, couldn't help it. She was so close to getting her hand out of the rope, but any more wiggling would likely draw attention to it, so she held still. "You don't approve of murder? You're a serial killer."

He shook his head. "I don't kill. I collect." He reached out, traced the shape of her eye with his finger. Quinn tried to pull away, but there was nowhere to go with the tree trunk behind her. "I'm not going to lie to you, Sarah. This is going to hurt. But I'm not going to kill you. I don't kill."

"You scoop people's eyeballs out and you think you don't kill?"

"My grandfather taught me how. How to do it right. It's my first memory. Grandpa's lap. Eyeballs. Blood. I have to make the collection complete for Mother."

He genuinely thought he wasn't a murderer. And who knew, with all these other Dunnes and then the grande dame of them all, maybe he didn't do the actual killing.

But that hardly made him the good guy.

"Listen to me, buddy, really listen. I don't know what your mother's told you, or your grandfather…" As a *child*, what a horror. "…but it's *all* wrong. You take my *eyes*, I'm a dead woman. And that is on your conscience."

Again he shook his head. "If I complete the collection, I win the game. I don't like to kill, so I don't have to. I just have to win."

"What do you win?" Because he kept talking about this game, his collection—which she had the terrifying suspicion was the eyeballs—but never about the *end*.

"I win," he repeated. "That's what I win. I win. I'm better than *your* Dunne, no matter what *she* says."

Quinn tried to keep her breathing even, no matter how much it tried to go ragged. "You want to beat my Dunne? That's it? Familial rivalry?"

He looked down at the tool in his hand. "His eyes are like mine, aren't they?"

Quinn shuddered. "What do you get if you beat him?"

"I don't want to talk anymore. I know this will hurt, but the pain can be good. Sometimes, pain makes you stronger. You only have to be brave and strong."

He lifted the tool and this time Quinn didn't bother to hide her thrashing. He'd likely assume she was just ineffectively moving around, but she was close...so close.

"Sit still," he muttered.

But she tossed her head back and forth as she wiggled her hand out of the bond of the rope.

"Dunne Two and Four, get over here and hold her face still."

Quinn inwardly swore. They were going to hold her down and she was *dead*. Just...dead.

No. No, she wouldn't give up until there was nothing left to give up. She managed to free her arm and reached out and grasped fake Dunne's wrist. He tried to wrench free, but she was stronger.

The problem was the two men with guns still calmly and casually walking toward her, with the guns pointed at her, ready to shoot. Clearly at fake Dunne's command.

"You can't take my eyes," she managed to grit out, gripping his arm as hard as she could.

He struggled with her grasp, but clearly wasn't *afraid.* "They'll only shoot you. Not to kill, of course. But enough I can get what I want. I always get what I want."

"They'll kill me. You know that. Deep down, I think you know they'll kill me no matter what you do with my eyes."

There was the slightest hesitation, his fight against her grip relaxing a little. "I'm not a murderer."

"Okay, I believe you. I believe you don't want to be." She had to get through to him somehow. Get him to see what he was actually doing. He was a victim too, sort of.

She'd gotten through everything in her life, up to meeting Jessie through sheer grit and brazenness.

But it looked like she was going to have to be a little sincere to get out of this one. "Dunne, I don't want to die. I don't even want to hurt you. I want us both to walk out of here in one piece. Us and *my* Dunne. Your mother doesn't want that. She wants us to die. So please. Don't do this."

DUNNE COULD NOT figure out what this *test* was going to entail, even as Sandy and the various Dunnes set things up.

They were creating a large space in the middle of the camp. The rain had slowed, the thunder and lightning tapering off to distant rumbles and flashes, but everything was a muddy, swampy mess.

This seemed to make Sandy happy, though she now sat on a camping chair on a strange little wooden platform, as if she had to stay out of the mud, like some kind of queen tended to by servants.

But Dunne was also happy, because if the storm blew out, then he knew Quinn would be back to her old self rather than the shaking, scared mess she'd been in the back of his truck. He didn't want that for her. Of course, he didn't want *any* of this for her.

Keeping his body still, he worked on getting his hands free of the ropes behind his back and behind the tree. He watched the goings-on, but no one seemed to pay much mind to him.

No, this was nothing like his time in the military, even the few times he'd had close calls with various terrorist cells. Everything had been clear—point A followed to point B, and even if he didn't agree with anyone's reasons for causing terror, for killing women and children, he could *follow* the reasoning in many of his targets' minds.

This? This in front of him was all lunacy. This made Quinn's family issues look like whimsical quirkiness. This felt like the kind of story people wouldn't even make a movie out of—too unbelievable, people would say.

But here he was, his aunt on a platform, men who were all named after him, cousins, essentially, born and bred to act as her little warped army. She had tests and theories about…his mother and him being perfect—or proving they weren't.

What would Quinn do in this situation? Stand here trying to free her arms and assess the situation? No, she'd act. She'd poke. He managed to get one arm a little free. A few more tugs and he'd have it. But he wanted Sandy distracted, reacting when he did it.

"This isn't genetics," he offered, trying to sound as bored as Quinn did when she was delivering annoying facts. "It's a choice."

Sandy's expression went cold as she fixed him with a glare. "What would you know about it?"

"I have a choice. My mother had a choice." It hurt to even think about his mother being connected to this. No wonder she let Dad sweep her away from her family, her life. If this was the alternative, he would take his father ten times over. At least Dad had loved her. "Everyone has a choice between right and wrong, and I know plenty of people who grew up with wrong and turned out all right." He thought of Quinn. She maybe didn't see herself that way, but he did. She hadn't stood a chance in hell of turning out normal, and God knew, she wasn't *normal* by any means, but there was some goodness in her. Some honor. A sense of what felt right, what felt wrong.

He got his hand free while Sandy yelled at one of the Dunnes for dropping something. With a little maneuvering, he'd be able to reach into his pocket and pull out his knife and cut the rest of the bonds away.

"You chose the wrong path, Sandy, because you wanted to," he said, watching the anger suffuse her face as he slowly moved his arm closer to his side. It was still technically bound by the rope, but with his hand free, he had a certain range of motion. Just a little bit more and he'd have the knife.

She stood on her platform, the chair clattering backward with the force of it. "I'm your aunt, you'll address me as such."

It'll be a cold day in hell. "You didn't have to kill anyone. You didn't *have* to follow in your father's footsteps." He tried one of Quinn's smirks. "My mother certainly didn't kill anyone. I'm not sure she ever even hurt anyone or said a bad word about anyone. She was good, through and through." He'd seen her all wrong, Dunne realized. Because he hadn't realized what a victim of her childhood circumstances she'd been.

"Because she always got everything!" Sandy said, enraged, like a toddler throwing a tantrum. "She could escape. No one would marry *me* and save me. No one would move *me* a continent away. I had no choices! There was only death! And you…you made those same choices."

She practically leapt off the platform, mud splashing up against her skirt as she strode across the campsite toward him, her eyes blazing with fury. She pointed at him. "You can dress it up in your father's military finery, but you've killed. You've taken lives. You've spilled blood. It's *in* you, Dunne. And I want it to come out."

It hurt, when he shouldn't let anything this woman said hurt, but…wasn't that what he'd worried about? For most of his military career, he'd been convinced he'd been doing the right thing, but as the missions to infiltrate terrorist organizations had led from one to another, all those groups convinced they were in the right too, Dunne had suffered a crisis of faith, of surety.

And he'd wondered, because murder was obviously in the blood, how much like his grandfather he was, deep down.

Sandy smirked at him. "You know it too. Excellent. That'll make this entire thing faster, easier. Once you break, Dunne, it will feel…like freedom. You can be free of anyone in your life you don't want, anyone in your way. Murder isn't a *choice* between right and wrong. It's power."

"What power do you have, spending your life camping in the woods, Sandy? Because last time I checked people in hiding weren't *free* or *powerful*."

Her mouth curled into another sneer. For a second, he thought she might backhand him. But she brought her hands slowly together in front of her instead. She laced her fingers and looked at him with cool disdain.

"The first part of the test is patience. Knowing the right moment to strike. Knowing your victim's *weakest* moment." She lifted his chin with her finger, and studied him as if considering. "You aren't there quite yet. But you will be."

Chapter Nineteen

Quinn bit her tongue to keep from talking. Fake Dunne was untying her. She didn't want to say *anything* to change that.

The two other Dunnes watched on with frowns, but they didn't mount any opposition. Per usual, they didn't speak at all.

He kept the rope around her wrists behind her back, but loosely. "They'll tighten if you try to run," he said. "But this will do to get where we need to go."

"Where's that?"

"To Mother. She hasn't given the signal, but clearly, I have some things to discuss with her."

He started to pull Quinn forward, not back where they'd originally come from but in a new direction. Quinn tried to study his profile and make out what this meant. She tried not to hope too hard for salvation here.

"So…you believe me?"

He stopped walking for a moment and regarded her with a faint frown. "I don't want to kill you."

Quinn nodded. She believed that, in a weird, warped way. But she also knew he *might* kill her. It was still a very real possibility. And if *he* didn't, anyone else could. Still, she wasn't about to say that to him when she was so close to being free. "I know."

"She always tells me I have to want to. It's the game, the test. She doesn't want me to, but she does. Mother doesn't always make sense."

Quinn shook her head, feeling overwhelmed with emotion. She'd been through some serious emotional manipulation as a child, but she'd finally met someone worse off than her. "You don't have to want to kill anyone, you don't have to hurt anyone. I promise you."

He looked at her again. "I do want your eyes."

Quinn couldn't hide her revulsion over that statement, and his mouth tightened, so she hurried to change the subject. Away from anything that might relate to her eyes. She might survive this, and he might be a victim of his mother, but things were decidedly not *right* in fake Dunne's mind.

"Do the Dunnes have to do what you say?" she asked, pointing to the two gunmen following them at a pace.

He glanced back at them. "More or less. Mother is the leader, but I'm second in command. I pass the test, but she wants me to lose the game."

Quinn thought about asking what that meant, but she decided the safer subject was the other Dunnes. "They don't get a say in anything?"

"They can't speak. Physically. When they failed, mother made sure they couldn't speak. They're lucky they have eyes, honestly." He shrugged. "It's for the best."

It was most assuredly not for the best, and now

Quinn felt badly for the gunmen too. None of them had ever stood a chance. And she'd once been in a similar place. She wasn't important to her father, to his cause. She'd been expected to be a good little cog in the machine to find the gold, subvert the government.

You stood a chance, even up against all that happened to you.

The thought sat uncomfortably on her shoulders, especially since it sounded like Dunne in her head, trying to tell her she was good enough when...

Well, it didn't do thinking about right now. She couldn't *pity* the men pointing guns at her back when she needed to escape them. Even if they'd been stripped of their ability to talk. Even if they didn't deserve to be here.

But she did pity them. All of them. And still, she had to find a way to survive this, and maybe if she did, they could all get the help they so desperately needed.

"My father used me in his pursuit of treasure," she offered. He'd humanized himself in a very warped way, so maybe if she did the same he would let her go with her eyeballs intact. "He was obsessed with this old gold that most people didn't think existed. It turned out he was right about the gold, but he didn't get any of it because he hurt and killed people along the way."

"Did you?" Fake Dunne asked with what seemed like genuine interest.

"I tried not to. Sometimes I had to, to protect myself. Never in the quest for that stupid gold," she said vehemently, then wondered why she was working so hard to defend herself to a man who scooped eyeballs out of living people. So maybe she wasn't so much defending herself to him…but to herself. "If someone was going to try to kill me or…other things, there was a few times I defended myself and someone ended up dead."

"Isn't it the same? If I take your eyes, and you end up dead, *I* didn't do it. *End up* is different than *murder*."

Quinn bit back a swear. Well, she'd walked herself into that one. She tried to think in terms he'd understand. Tried to remind herself to talk to him as though he were a rational human being, even if he wasn't. "Have I hurt you, Dunne? Have I tried to kill you? Or did I just run away when you captured me?"

He was quiet for a while, and they walked through the woods. She was so cold from the wet that she was basically numb at this point. Except her leg, which alternately felt like it was on fire or that it wouldn't hold her up for the next step…but it always did.

"And *my* Dunne hasn't done anything to you either. He could have. When you had me in that net. He had a shot, but the only good one would have been fatal. So he didn't take it. Even though he wanted to save me, he couldn't bring himself to take it."

Still, fake Dunne remained quiet.

"We're the good guys, Dunne," she said. She probably never would have believed in including herself in a group of *good guys*, but she was definitely better than what fake Dunne was a part of.

Fake Dunne stopped fully and came to stand in front of her. He studied her face with a kind of detached gaze. "What does it matter if we're good or bad?"

Quinn opened her mouth, but she had no answer for

that. What did it matter? "I don't know," she managed to say, though her throat was tight. She thought about Jessie and Sarabeth. Her family, her real family, because they loved and cared about her long before they'd had any reason to. "I guess it's about…what you can live with. I can't live with being someone who hurts people, who causes harm just because I can."

He shrugged. "I can. And your Dunne will lose the game. Mother makes everyone lose. Except me. I'm stronger. That's what you've made me see, Sarah. I'm better."

Quinn closed her eyes as the wave of defeat threatened to take the last bit of strength she had. A tear slipped over her cheek.

"Why are you crying?" he asked, still sounding vaguely curious and mostly unmoved.

"Because I thought you understood. I thought I could reach you. I thought there was something decent inside you, Dunne."

When he only looked confused, she realized there was only one real way out of this. She focused on planting her feet, on the space she'd have to create to put distance between herself and the two men who held guns but couldn't talk.

"There's no point in getting emotional," he responded. "You were right. Mother wants you to die. Mother is the murderer. We have to stop her."

"And then what?"

Fake Dunne shrugged. "I'll still need to finish my collection, of course, but it doesn't *have* to be you. It could be Mother." He nodded as if thinking it over and coming to an agreeable conclusion. "Yes, it could be her. Her eyes are brown, sort of like yours. It could work. And you understand, so you can take her place."

"Take her place?" Quinn echoed, feeling light-headed and sure she'd misheard him.

"Yes, you always need at least one woman around. How else could there be more Dunnes?"

More… "Oh no. You've got this mixed up, buddy. There will be no Dunnes coming out of me."

He shrugged. "We'll see."

She was going to keep arguing, but then thought better of it. For the moment. "And what happens to Dunne when that happens?"

His expression hardened, sharpened. "*I* am Dunne. The only Dunne who matters." He cocked his head and studied her. Then reached out and traced around her eye again even as she jerked away.

Oh, *hell* no. This was it. This was her one and only moment.

Quinn charged.

DUNNE KNEW HE couldn't stay here much longer. He was wearing down. Tired. Dehydrated. His leg wouldn't hold him up if he didn't get out of this and soon.

He'd gotten his knife from his pants, but he was struggling to get the right angle to cut himself out, and even if he did accomplish the goal, he'd have to be ready to fight off six men with guns and one very unbalanced woman.

They were still in "patience" mode, apparently. He

doubted it was a test and figured it was more…something else.

They were waiting on something or someone. Did he really want to be here when it showed up?

No. No, it was time to get this over with.

He wrenched his arm—it sent a pain cascading throughout his body, and it drew the attention of Sandy and a few of the Dunnes with guns, but they didn't move forward, and now he had the angle to get the blade to the rope.

"Even if you escape, we have six men with guns to chase you down and shoot you."

"Doesn't sound like much of a test or game if you just shoot me."

"Shooting doesn't have to equal death, Dunne. I thought you, Mr. Military, would know that."

Clearly she had no idea how intimately he knew that. Even now his leg throbbed—the pain was so bad it reminded him of those first excruciating days of rehab. Would it even hold him up if he ran?

Or would the gunman get the exact kind of shot off that would leave him out of commission for another year or so? If he was lucky.

Dunne weighed his options. The sun was rising, so he couldn't use the cover of darkness to help him if he needed to run. He didn't think Sandy had plans to kill him, or Quinn for that matter, but she certainly wasn't going to treat them *well*. Games and tests, torture no doubt.

"You're really just going to follow her blindly? Like

mindless robots?" he asked the man closest to him. The *Dunne* closest to him.

"They can't answer you, of course," Sandy replied. "They didn't pass the test. So they got a number and lost their tongues. They're soldiers, but they aren't people. You know the feeling, don't you? Maybe you'll fail the test and end up with them. You're an expert at it."

She certainly knew how to aim an arrow at his insecurities from those old hurts, but something about her trying to twist them around on him had him facing them head-on instead of shying away.

"I was a soldier. I killed people, and yeah, sometimes I had some doubts in retrospect about if I'd done the right thing. There are always regrets when it comes to war." And weren't those regrets what had kept him holed up in the room at the ranch, avoiding settling into *life*? He'd been surviving, just like Quinn.

Because his leg was injured, because his life's purpose was taken away from him, because he didn't know who to be if he had to face the fact that he hadn't been the perfect soldier…and didn't want to try to be anymore, even if he could have.

There'd been a relief in his injury, in being erased. He'd been ready to be done, because he knew that parts of what he'd been doing were right, or necessary, but he also knew it wasn't so simple. So black-and-white.

Ranch life was, but he'd settled in to the gray area of keeping himself held back. Of focusing his efforts on this whole Eye Socket Killer thing.

There'd been flashes of light, and he'd shied away from them. Jake and Zara getting engaged. The way

Henry was wrapped around Sarabeth's finger like he'd been born to be her father. The seasons on the ranch, the small town life that wanted to bring the Thompson brothers into the fold.

He'd been afraid, and now he didn't know *why*. This in front of him was a reason to be afraid. Life wasn't.

He didn't know why that made him think of Quinn. Leaning into him when she was afraid of the storm. *All* that innuendo she thought was so funny. How much he wanted her to believe that her past didn't change the way anyone saw her in the here and now. The way her lips had been close enough to kiss, and he'd wanted to. *Wanted to.*

But stopped himself from taking the leap.

For what? To end up here. Tied to a tree while his insane aunt built games and tests and threatened injury but not death. All wrapped up in some family drama that really had nothing to do with him, even if this woman had named all her children after him. That was her deal. This was all…hers. His grandfather's.

Now he knew who was killing people and he could turn all that over to the authorities who could handle it. Maybe he'd have to finagle that to not give away his real identity, but with Landon's help, he could do it.

He didn't have to take this on. He'd never had to. Everyone had pointed that out to him, but it wasn't until it was Quinn involved that it had resonated. Because with his brothers, he'd watched them all move on, except Cal, and Dunne hadn't been ready. So no matter what they said, he couldn't take it on board.

But Quinn had survived worse than him, and wasn't

that far removed from the hell she'd been in, and even she thought life was a better option.

So, there was absolutely no point to staying here. Trying to dismantle it. Life was the answer.

He cut more vigorously, and as their attention had gone to the woods, they didn't even notice the movement. He got his arms free and was ready to run when he realized they were focused on the sounds of people coming. Loudly.

The man with the Eye-owa plates appeared through the trees. Along with the two gunman who'd taken Quinn away.

He waited, but Quinn didn't appear. She wasn't with them.

For a moment his heart soared. She'd escaped.

Then he had the terrible realization.

Or she was dead. Because the man's nose was bleeding, but he was here. Bloodied, but here. The two gunmen were unharmed and here.

And Quinn wasn't.

Chapter Twenty

Quinn's charge had knocked fake Dunne off his feet, and possibly broke his nose if the *crunch* and screaming were anything to go by. She had figured skull to nose was her best option. She hoped to God she was right.

But she didn't stick around to find out or fight. She ran like hell. She didn't care where she ended up as long as it was far, far away from the possibility of creating *more* Dunnes with fake Dunne.

She'd made a mistake feeling sorry for him. Maybe at some point in the future, if her and real Dunne survived, she would. But in this moment? She couldn't get through to him, not the way she thought she had.

So she ran. If they shot at her, she didn't hear it. If they followed, she had no idea. Never in her life had she run with absolutely no plan, or with such whole-body panic. She barely even noticed her hands still tied behind her. Her only endgame was to get as far away as possible as quickly as possible.

She dodged rocks and trees, nearly sobbing as her leg threatened to give out, but adrenaline must have kept her upright.

Until she ran into the hard wall of something. Painfully. Jarringly.

But it wasn't something. It was some*one*. Because they reached out and kept her from falling to the ground. Then held on.

She fought like hell, even with her arms tied around her back. She used her legs, her head. No one was going to take her. No one—

But the sharp order and her real name had her head whipping up. It nearly bashed into a very strong, very familiar chin. "Cal," she breathed. Cal. Cal.

There was *backup*.

So, she just started…crying, her leg finally giving out, though Cal held her upright. God, she didn't even care how weak that made her. Cal was here. Oh God, they were saved. "How did you find us?" she sobbed into his chest.

He patted her shoulder awkwardly, clearly taken aback and very uncomfortable with her reaction. "When we couldn't get a response from either of you, we figured out you came to Nebraska. We couldn't figure out where, beyond the town, until a few hours ago when we finally got a ping off Dunne's phone."

She pulled back from his chest again. "Dunne. Did you find him? Where is he? Is he okay?"

"Turn around," Cal ordered, and she was so out of sorts she followed instruction without hesitation.

Cal cut the ropes off her hands and regarded her with a slightly terrified suspicion. "Who are you and what have you done with Quinn?"

"Ha ha. Where is real *Dunne*?"

He frowned at her but didn't question *real*. He took her arm and started pulling her in a direction—she didn't know which one. She didn't even care, because she was...

Saved. She was okay.

"We've got a circle going on," Cal explained. "We're slowly moving in, making sure we don't miss him. He wasn't at the exact ping, so we're still searching."

"Okay." Quinn swallowed. *Still searching.* "You haven't come across anyone yet?"

"Your stampeding-elephant impersonation was my first sign of someone."

Quinn only nodded, not responding to his commentary on her running at all. She didn't know what to say. So many emotions were ricocheting around inside of her and she couldn't seem to marshal them into the acceptable compartments.

She should be old hat at this kind of thing, but she was all jumbled, because Dunne was still in danger. Because just like the whole thing at the end with her family, someone she cared about was involved.

She'd saved Jessie. It was up to her to save Dunne. But Cal's grip on her arm tightened.

"All right, you are acting *so* weird. I'm taking you back to the truck."

"What? No." She tried to jerk her arm away, but Cal's grip didn't loosen. "I know where he is." She looked around. "Sort of."

"Quinn, you're on your last legs. Let me take you back to the truck and then—"

"Last legs is better than no legs. Or eyes." She shuddered.

Cal winced. "You guys found the eye-murderer guy?"

"He wanted my eyes." God, she wanted to close her eyes, maybe pass out, let Cal take her to the truck. But Dunne was still out there. "It's not just one guy or killer. It's a bunch. There's this woman, and then there are all these men. The Dunnes can't talk, except the Dunne without a number."

"Quinn," he said, and there was a soft but censuring note to his voice. She'd never once heard Cal be *soft* about anything, except maybe Sarabeth.

She looked up at him and realized… "You don't believe me. You think I'm…like wounded and addled or something."

"I can't make sense of what you're saying *to* believe you. I genuinely think you need to get back to the truck. We'll get you to a doctor as soon as we find Dunne."

She shook her head. "I'm not explaining myself well because it's all so weird, but I'm okay. I have to help him. We have to stop her."

"Okay. Let's clarify. Who has Dunne?"

"This woman. And six men, all named Dunne. They have guns, but they can't speak and they do whatever the woman says. And I ran away from a man, fake Dunne, and he had two gunmen with him who can't speak, who just do whatever he says."

She could tell he wasn't sure about her—mentally or otherwise, but he was pulling her forward and she had to pray it wasn't toward the truck. She needed to help.

"Eight gunmen," Cal said. "A woman and another man, as well, but they're unarmed?"

"They don't *appear* to have guns, but they're so unstable I can't predict what they might do. They're definitely dangerous, guns or not."

Cal pulled a walkie-talkie–looking thing out of his pocket and relayed the information.

"Is everyone here?"

"The brothers."

Quinn nodded. That still left them a little shorthanded, but seven against ten was way better than the original two against ten. As long as Dunne wasn't hurt. Still, six against ten was doable. She'd dealt with worse odds.

"When they had me, they tied me to a tree. But I was a prize for the game. Dunne was a player, I think. Or he had to pass a test? It's all so confusing." She pressed her hand to her forehead where a spiking pain had lodged itself. She needed food, water, but first she needed Dunne. *My Dunne*.

"Well, we'll find him. Reasons don't really matter."

Quinn didn't agree with that, but she appreciated the way Cal moved. He was being careful, stealthy, his eyes tracked everywhere. It was all very Dunne-like... or she supposed, military-like.

"They don't want to kill him. At least, not right off, but...it's all a plot. A plan. So we have to be careful. They wanted him to come here. I think we figured things out quicker than they expected. They weren't ready right away, but they wanted him to come here. That was the endgame."

Cal slid her a look, and she couldn't read it. Or tell what he meant by it when his words were flat. "You mean *you* figured things out quicker than they expected."

Her foot hit the ground funny and she nearly crumpled, but Cal held her up and waited for her to get her feet under her again. She could sense his speculation. Knew he wanted to take her back to the truck. So, she had to find some semblance of her usual self. To prove to him she had to be here.

She had to be here.

"Glad my understanding of culty leaders and their unbalanced plotting can come in handy."

"You should be glad. What if this had happened months ago? Before we knew you? What if he'd gone on the exact wild-goose chase they were hoping for?"

Quinn blinked at that. Cal was giving her…credit? "I don't want to think about that," she managed.

"Neither do I. So let's—"

But then a gunshot exploded through the woods.

And both Quinn and Cal ran toward it.

DUNNE HAD CUT the ropes away from his hands behind the tree, but he held them back as if he was still tied, while Sandy and fake Dunne faced off.

"Where is she?" Sandy demanded.

Fake Dunne raised his chin. "I decided to let her go," he said loftily. Obviously the blood dripping from his nose spoke to a completely different outcome, but she was alive or he'd say he'd killed her.

Dunne nearly sagged with relief. She had gotten out.

He knew she'd do something stupid like try to come back for him, but for the time being, she was safe from his family of insane people.

"You let her *go*," Sandy repeated, with a frigid calm that had even Dunne bracing himself for some kind of explosion. "What would possess you to make that kind of decision on your own?"

Fake Dunne eyed her coolly. "I'm not a murderer, Mother. I don't like to kill. I'm tired of you trying to turn me into one."

"You don't understand what I'm trying to do," Sandy shot back.

Dunne surveyed his options. Part of him wondered if he could simply melt into the woods while they fought. Sure, one of the Dunnes with guns might get a shot off, but they'd have to notice him.

He looked at each of them. They were all looking at Sandy. He moved his leg, just a test to see if a step in another direction might garner someone's attention.

"We needed her!" Sandy exploded. "Grab him. Grab him!"

Dunne was about to take a step backward, quickly melt into the trees, but Sandy pointed at him. "And him. It's time. If he didn't bring the girl, he'll have to do it himself."

Dunne could have run. He considered it. But his leg wouldn't have allowed him to get very far. He could have fought the two Dunnes who approached him, but there didn't seem to be much of a point. More would come.

He had to keep waiting it out. They'd make a mistake. He had to believe they'd make a mistake that allowed him to get out of here before Quinn came busting in and got herself even more hurt than she already was.

Two Dunnes pulled him into the center of the large circle they'd cleared not seeming to care that his ties had already been cut while two other ones pulled fake Dunne into the circle as well. They faced each other as the Dunnes fell back and created a circle around them, guns pointed.

Sandy took a deep breath as if centering herself. "This is the test. One of you will kill the other," she announced as if explaining what was going to be served for lunch. "There's no other way of getting out of here. If you both fail, you'll both die."

Fake Dunne rolled his eyes. "You're not going to kill me, Mother. I'm special."

"You'll break! You'll both break! You're like me and you'll break! You can't help it. It's in you."

Dunne watched her scream and stomp. "I won't kill him," he stated firmly. Then turned to fake Dunne. "I'm not going to kill you."

"One of you will break!" Sandy screamed.

Fake Dunne regarded him, as if thinking the whole thing over. Calmly. Rationally. But there was nothing rational about this man. "I suppose if I was going to kill anyone, it'd be you."

"I'm not going to kill anyone here," Dunne repeated. He knew he would kill to save if he had to, but it'd be a last resort. Never a first choice.

Fake Dunne kept staring at him. "You have my eyes. I could add my eyes to my collection, and wouldn't that be fun?"

"Yes, Dunne," Sandy said, talking to fake Dunne. "Don't you see? If you kill him, you get everything you want. Whatever eyes your heart desires. You just have to prove to me that you're like us. Not just the eyes, but you have to take a life. You have to experience it to *truly* be special."

Fake Dunne shot a petulant look at Sandy. "I *am* special." He turned back to Dunne. "Our grandfather taught me. He showed me how. He wanted me to be just like him. Not you."

"Fine by me," Dunne muttered.

"We aren't like them because we don't feel the need to kill," Fake Dunne said, gesturing at the circle of gunmen around them. "But you killed in the military, so I'm not like you. I've never killed. *I* am special."

"Congratulations."

Fake Dunne sneered. "But *she* always talked about *you*. And your mother. Like you were something special, but *I'm* the special one."

"All I know is I don't have a collection of eyeballs, buddy." Dunne eyed the spacing between the Dunnes with guns. Could he effectively bolt? If Fake Dunne was supposed to kill him, would they even be allowed to shoot?

"All right. How do you want me to do it, Mother?" He turned to the Dunne behind him. "Give me your gun."

That Dunne handed it over without a pause. Well, this was not good. He'd have to—

But he heard an odd…noise. Not quite a whistle but not…*not* a whistle.

An old military signal. An old plan.

Rescue. As long as he didn't get close-range *shot* in the next few seconds.

But before he could be too relieved, Quinn stepped into the little circle. She was too pale, ragged and a mess. But her eyes flashed defiance. "Hey, guys. Remember me?

Chapter Twenty-One

"What the hell are you doing, Quinn?" Dunne seethed.

But that was *really* the wrong thing to say because fake Dunne looked at her, gun still in his hands and ready to shoot. "You said your name was *Sarah*. You lied to me? You hurt me and—"

The gun kept moving, closer and closer to being aimed at her. Yeah, time for backup. Quinn whistled and then…all hell broke loose.

Shots fired. People running. Fighting. Since she wasn't armed, and she knew the Thompson brothers well enough to know their nobility would get in the way, Quinn went for the woman.

She didn't seem to have a weapon, because she was trying to run into the woods. *Yeah right*.

Quinn's leg might hurt like the devil, and she was tired, definitely, as Cal had put it, on her last legs. But she would be *damned* if this woman escaped.

Quinn quickly realized with her leg holding her back she wasn't going to be able to catch up…unless she made a leaping, lunging tackle. She didn't have much time to do it or the woman would put enough distance between them to avoid it, so she simply…flung her body toward the retreating woman.

Quinn landed in a tangle of excruciating pain, hard ground, but also the limbs of someone else. So, she grabbed—for arms, for legs, for anything to keep this woman pinned to the ground.

The woman howled—whether in pain or anger, Quinn had no idea, but Quinn fought her with all she had. Because this woman was the mastermind of everything and she needed to *pay*.

"*You* made them all this way." It flowed through her, an anger and an emotional tide of vengeance that maybe wasn't *all* about this woman and had to do a little bit with her own issues, but still…

"It's not my fault! It's *never* been my fault!" The woman landed a hard kick to Quinn's bad leg that had Quinn's eyes watering and her gasping in pain.

But Quinn held on. She didn't let the woman wriggle away. They fought. Quinn punched. The woman elbowed.

"You're not a part of this," the woman screeched, breathing heavily as she tried to scratch Quinn's face. Quinn managed to whip her head around and knock the woman's hand away.

"Your *son* kidnapped me. He wanted my eyes. Because you let him. You made him. You both made me a part of this, and you're both going to pay."

"He's like us. He's one of us. He's going to break. They're all going to break!"

Even as she grappled with the woman, she had to

come to the sad conclusion that her father hadn't been really insane. He'd been terrible, no doubt, but he'd been a selfish, mean kind of terrible. He'd understood reality though. Maybe he'd been a little delusional about his own power, but who wasn't?

This woman? She was legitimately, lights-out insane. And Quinn had to stop her before she hurt anyone else. She tried to grab the woman's arms, but couldn't quite get a grasp on either wrist.

Then suddenly, for no reason Quinn could discern, the woman went completely still. She looked Quinn right in the eye.

"I'm going to kill you," the woman said. And she was *so* still now. Calm. Quinn hesitated for just a second, because the woman had…given up, but then said that, and—

But then Dunne was there, because of course he was. He somehow just sort of pulled her up and basically tossed her out of the way. She landed with a thud on the ground, her vision blurring and spinning for a second.

As her sight settled, she realized that Sandy had somehow gotten a gun—a small, almost unnoticeable one, but Dunne had seen it.

And he'd gotten her out of the way, but as he gripped the gun and tried to pry it from the woman's grasp, it exploded. He jerked, stumbled back.

"No!"

He fell, and for a blinding moment of terror, nothing else mattered. Quinn had to get to him. Just him. Just… He had to be okay. She didn't think about the woman. She didn't care about the gun. She didn't think about anything except him.

She crawled over to him, her hands wildly looking for the bullet wound. "No one takes bullets for me, you idiot," she said, realizing belatedly tears were falling and maybe she was sobbing, and for as rough as she'd had it, she'd certainly never cried so much in front of people in her *life*.

"Where'd it hit you?" she demanded, forgetting about everything else. He wasn't lying on the ground. He was in a sitting position, sort of holding his arm, the gun he'd taken from the woman next to him.

He didn't answer though, and she ran her hands all over him, finding nothing. But he was just sitting there. Sitting there. Oh God. Her head was just a panicked, whirling buzz and she touched his face. With her fingers, with her lips. She kissed his forehead. "Please be okay," she said, something like a chant.

She could feel his pulse. He was alive. *Alive*. And the relief was just…overpowering. It completely obliterated any rational thought, because she pressed her mouth to his.

Alive. Alive. Dunne is alive.

And he kissed her back, but… Wait.

She pulled away as his words finally penetrated. Because he *was* responding, was talking. Had been.

Quinn, I am okay. Had he been saying that the whole time? She swallowed, trying to shake the ringing in her head away.

His arm was bleeding, but when she took the time

to see, to *think,* even she knew it wasn't more than a flesh wound. He really was okay…and she'd just fallen all over him like some kind of… She'd *kissed* him.

He kind of kissed you back.

Right, like some sort of reflex, she was sure. What an embarrassment. She looked around. The Thompson brothers had tied everyone up and were putting tourniquets on those who'd been shot.

They were going to survive, so now she had to live with what she'd done.

But not yet.

DUNNE'S ARM BURNED, and his leg throbbed, but he was okay, and all the other Dunnes—he still shuddered at the thought—were handled.

Landon and Henry came over to help him to his feet. Quinn stepped away. Farther and farther away, like she wanted distance from *him.*

She'd kissed him. Sure, in a panicked desperation, but that wasn't exactly the *normal* panic or desperation response. Crying? Sure. Kissing?

Well…

Cal spoke to Quinn in low tones, but Dunne overheard. Words that didn't make sense. "What are you doing?" Dunne demanded. Of Cal. Of Quinn.

"I've got this. The cops are going to come and I'm going to deal with the fallout." She glanced at him once, but only once. "I'm the kidnap victim who escaped the murderers. You guys disappear so your identities aren't looked into. Sure, my whole not having an ID will be a little problematic, but better than you guys getting wrapped up in something that connects to your actual family and has people asking questions about Dunne Wilks."

Dunne tried to take a step toward her, but Landon's grip was firm. "There's no—"

But he was cut off by one of her patented derisive waves. "Already decided when we swept in to save you, Dunne. I stay. You go."

Dunne glared at Cal. "You can't be serious."

"It was her idea, but it's not a bad one."

"Who'll believe you took them all down on your own?" Dunne demanded, pointing to ten tied-up people in varying shades of beaten up. "They won't back up your story. The ones who can talk."

Quinn rolled her eyes. "Trust me. I'm *very* convincing, and who's going to believe anything this group says?"

Landon handed him off to Jake. Then he shrugged off his backpack. "You've got ID," he said to Quinn. "Papers. Everything you need. I made sure of it." Landon pulled a large envelope out of his bag. "I'll give you the license, and a few other things it might make sense to have on your person, but that's it. We'll have the rest back at the ranch if the cops want to dig for more. I'm going to hack into the motel records and have your real name put on the room. You came here to do a hike by yourself. If the lady at the desk mentions Dunne checking in with you, you just explain he was a…"

"One-night stand?" Quinn suggested with a smirk.

Landon looked back at Dunne, and whatever he saw in Dunne's expression had him biting back a retort other than, "Sure."

Dunne turned to Cal, because Cal was always in charge and this was inexcusable. "You can't leave her here."

"The cops are coming. She's right. We can't be here."

"They all know we were here," he said, pointing to the group of people who were somehow his family. Somehow this…warped.

"Trust me," Quinn said again. "It'll be easy to convince the cops they're delusional, since, you know, they are. I can say they turned on each other. Go. Before they get here."

"Quinn—"

"I've got this," she repeated, and her eyes were fierce. Her jaw set and stubborn. There was no way of talking her out of it. No way.

So he had to walk away. There wasn't another option that didn't put his brothers at risk. His father at risk. He had to protect the Dunne Thompson identity at all costs.

But he wasn't just…walking away.

"Let me go," Dunne muttered, jerking his arm from Jake. "Bum leg, but I can damn well walk."

His brothers exchanged glances, but they said nothing as he stalked…or limped…over to Quinn. She lifted her chin, everything in her expression and posture daring him to argue some more.

So, he didn't. He took her by the shoulders, and then pressed his mouth to hers. It wasn't the crazed desperation of her please-be-okay kiss, but maybe it was tinged with his frustration over leaving her here. To clean up *his* mess…which was all she seemed to do.

He pulled back, and he wasn't sure how long he stared at the shock on her face, on the woman who'd saved him again and again, in a lot of different ways. He'd never dreamed he could shock her, so he'd take that as a win.

"If this doesn't go exactly as planned, I'm pulling you out. I don't care what happens. You're not back in Wilde in forty-eight hours, I'm dragging you back myself."

She let out a shuddery breath. "Tempting."

But it didn't sound like *her* with that shuddery breath before it, and that was something, he supposed.

Because she was right, unfortunately, *again*. There was no way of getting out of this without the military getting involved. And if Quinn dealt with the cops… His brothers and all their identities were safe.

"Come on," Cal said. "We've got to go. They're on their way."

So he let himself be dragged out of the woods, while Quinn was left to clean up his mess.

But the long hike back to Cal's truck parked on the side of the highway—so the cops didn't see it in any of the refuge parking lots—Dunne came to the conclusion that… When someone jumped in to help, to clean up your mess, to take care of things for you…

It wasn't such a bad thing. It was an *I have your back* thing. For years, his brothers had had his back, and he'd had theirs.

Now…they had more than just each other.

And that was something to lean into.

Chapter Twenty-Two

Quinn couldn't remember the last time she'd been so tired. Jessie had driven out to Nebraska to pick her up after the cops had questioned her and medics had checked her out.

The cops had been skeptical, no doubt. But the evidence piled up in her favor. There'd been some questions about how she'd beaten them all, but they believed Quinn's rational one-at-a-time explanation over the woman—Sandy—ranting about *another* Dunne.

With Sandy and Fake Dunne ranting about games and tests and *all* the Dunnes without tongues, law enforcement had eventually come to the conclusion that even if Quinn was exaggerating, or lying about some things, it had nothing on those who were clearly mentally unstable.

She'd spent the night in the same motel she and Dunne had checked into, the proprietress no doubt chilly with the cops because she was hiding petty criminals. But it worked in Quinn's favor.

Somehow, everything worked in her favor. She answered their questions again in the morning until they were satisfied enough to let her go home. They'd seemed to expect her to call someone to pick her up, and since she was trying to play the victim here, she'd called Jessie.

Quinn had no doubt the police would contact her again, with more questions, and who-knew what all else. But they were letting her go home, and that was all she wanted.

Quinn doubted Sandy or her Dunnes would face any criminal charges. They all needed deep, psychological help. But that was the police's job to sort out, and she had no doubt Cal would keep tabs on it.

As for Quinn, she was done. She hoped Dunne felt the same way. They'd waded in. Stopped the killing. The rest… It wasn't theirs.

So, Jessie had come, and now she was on her way home. Jessie chatted a little bit but mostly let Quinn doze and didn't demand answers. She seemed content to simply drive them home.

Home.

Weird to think of the ranch as home simply because she'd been away a few days.

When Jessie finally pulled into the ranch, Quinn's stomach tightened into knots. She didn't want to face Dunne. She didn't want him to… Well, he was going to make it weird. And she'd have to face him like he didn't matter. She'd have to brazen it out.

And she just didn't have the energy. Not yet. She needed some time to…shore up her defenses. He'd… thank her. She had no doubt there'd be some dumb guilt speech she wanted no part of. Then he'd either bring up the kiss and do something obnoxious like apologize or, worse, try to let her down gently.

No. Way.

"I think I want to sleep for a week," Quinn announced when the car came to a stop. She got out and tried to bite back a hiss of pain. She'd had to hide her previous wound from the medic, and that had taken some doing.

It probably needed to be checked out, but she wasn't about to let Dunne look at her now. Or ever. She'd go to town for a real doctor. She had ID finally. Maybe no medical insurance, but she had money. She didn't need the down-low medical treatment from a gruff combat medic she wanted to kiss again.

Because *nope*, that had been a moment of weakness and she wasn't weak. She refused to be.

"Maybe Dunne should check out your leg," Jessie said, coming around the hood of the car to help her up the porch stairs.

"Nap first. Medic said I'm all good," Quinn lied. "Just rest and food and stuff."

Sarabeth appeared from the stables and came racing across the yard, so Quinn managed to distract Jessie by telling Sarabeth simplified but overdramatized versions of the army of Dunnes, all the way up to her room.

They stayed with her awhile, and no one else came up—thank God, really. She didn't want to see anyone else.

When she finally chased them away, she crawled into bed. She'd sleep and then… Well, they'd see.

QUINN WAS AVOIDING HIM. Dunne was certain of it. She'd been back two full days and he hadn't seen her once. She didn't come to meals, and if he casually questioned Jessie, she'd just given him an unreadable look and said Quinn was "resting."

He'd sunk so low as to try to surreptitiously ask Sarabeth about Quinn, but that girl was too smart for her own good.

If you want to talk to her so bad, why don't you stop asking about her and do something? We all live in the same dumb house.

She was right, of course, but it was complicated because there *were* so many people in this same dumb house.

But when he overheard Jessie say something to Henry about Quinn being out at the Peterson House, and Jessie being worried, Dunne was the first to offer to drive over and make sure she was okay.

He got some knowing looks, but he was past caring at this point.

The Peterson house was an old ranch home that had been abandoned by Jessie and Quinn's grandfather years ago and was now a falling-apart mess. But Quinn and Jessie had inherited the ruins and the ranch land last month when their father's estate had been settled out.

She was standing in front of it, looking at it. She turned, likely at the sound of his truck and frowned. Then frowned even deeper when he got out and walked over to her.

"What are you doing here?" She looked at him warily,

her hands shoved into her pockets. Like he was some kind of enemy.

He couldn't for the life of him think of why she'd think that, but he'd come here to say his piece.

"Jessie mentioned she was worried, and since you've been avoiding me, I figured it'd be a good place to have a private conversation."

"Pass," she replied, turning her scowl to the dilapidated ranch house. No windows. Caved roof. What she saw in there, he didn't know. He didn't know a lot when it came to Quinn.

But he wanted to.

"Quinn, I wanted to thank you."

She shook her head vigorously. "Whatever. I saved you. You saved me. Thank-yous are dumb and I don't want to get them or give them."

"Fine," he replied. He shoved his own hands in his pockets. How did she make him feel so damn awkward? "Cal says they're all going to be psychologically evaluated and we'll keep tabs on them. Sandy had quite the operation. Supplying false information to the media, moving bodies, hacking into the police files to create the location confusion on the pictures and creating the clues. But it's basically over and cleaned up."

"Great."

She said nothing, and he could have left it at that. He could have said anything else, but all that came out was an accusation. "You kissed me."

She froze, and there was the little flicker of *something* in her expression that had him realizing she was making him awkward on purpose. Because *she* was uncomfortable and wanted to feel like they were on equal footing.

She shrugged, but it was jerky. "It was a heat-of-the-moment thing. But we're fine now, so, like, don't apologize or make it weird."

But she kept her head down, not meeting his gaze. There was a defensiveness in the set of her shoulders. She wasn't *unmoved* or *uninterested*, she was…scared. No, not scared. Uncertain, which for her probably felt like scared.

"I won't make it weird," he said softly, then crossed the space she'd left between them. He reached out, his fingertips brushing along her jaw, then settling underneath her chin. He tilted it up, so she had no choice but to look at him.

He could see the internal fight on her face. To be herself. It was hard won, but she did it. She met his gaze with her haughty one. But he'd seen the fight. He understood her a little better now.

"Are you free tonight?"

Everything on her face scrunched into confusion. "Huh?"

"For dinner."

"What?"

"I'm asking you out on a date, Quinn."

She blinked. "A date."

"A date," he agreed. Trying not to smile. If she knew he was amused, she'd probably punch him. Why he liked that… Well, he probably didn't need to dissect it.

"Just…you and me?" she asked, a mix of suspicion and something…very different in her tone.

"Yes, dates are usually two people."

She swallowed. She opened her mouth, closed it. Then she blinked up at him, a lot of her masks falling away.

"It sounds so normal," she said, almost on a whisper. Like she was afraid to hope for normal.

He brought his other hand up to cup her face, because he understood that feeling *so* well. "I think at the very least we both deserve a lot of normal from here on out."

She studied his face for a very long time. When she finally answered, it was on that same whisper. "Okay."

He grinned at her. Yeah, it was going to be okay. "Okay."

She wrinkled her nose. "But not *too* normal, right?"

He laughed, winding his arm around her shoulders and pulling her into him. Where she liked to be. "With you? Never."

* * * * *

#2145 HER BRAND OF JUSTICE
A Colt Brothers Investigation • by B.J. Daniels
Ansley Brookshire's quest to uncover the truth about her adoption leads her to Lonesome, Montana—and into the arms cowboy Buck Crawford. But someone doesn't want the truth to come out...and will do *anything* to halt Ansley and Buck's search. Even kill.

#2146 TRAPPED IN TEXAS
The Cowboys of Cider Creek • by Barb Han
With a deadly stalker closing in, rising country star Raelynn Simmons needs to stay off the stage—and off the grid. Agent Sean Hayes accepts one last mission to keep her safe from danger. But with flying bullets putting them in close proximity, who will keep Sean's heart safe from Raelynn?

#2147 DEAD AGAIN
Defenders of Battle Mountain • by Nichole Severn
Macie Barclay never stopped searching for her best friend's murderer...until a dead body and a new lead reunites her with her ex, Detective Riggs Karig. Riggs knows he and Macie are playing with fire. Especially when she becomes the killer's next target...

#2148 WYOMING MOUNTAIN MURDER
Cowboy State Lawmen • by Juno Rushdan
Charlie Sharp knows how to defend herself. But when a client goes missing—presumed dead—she must rely on Detective Brian Bradshaw to uncover the truth. As they dig for clues and discover more dead bodies, all linked to police corruption, can they learn to trust each other to survive?

#2149 OZARKS DOUBLE HOMICIDE
Arkansas Special Agents • by Maggie Wells
A grisly double homicide threatens Michelle Fraser's yearslong undercover assignment. But the biggest threat to the FBI agent is Lieutenant Ethan Scott. He knows the seemingly innocent attorney is hiding something. But when they untangle a political money laundering conspiracy, how far will he go to keep Michelle's secrets?

#2150 DANGER IN THE NEVADA DESERT
by Denise N. Wheatley
Nevada's numeric serial killer is on a rampage—and his crimes are getting personal. When Sergeant Charlotte Bowman teams up with Detective Miles Love to capture the deranged murderer before another life is lost, they must fight grueling, deadly circumstances...and their undeniable attraction.

HICNM0423

HARLEQUIN
PLUS

Try the best multimedia subscription service for romance readers like you!

Read, Watch and Play.

Experience the easiest way to get the romance content you crave.

Start your **FREE TRIAL** at
<u>www.harlequinplus.com/freetrial</u>.